MONSTERS

PAINTED SMILES

MONSTERS
PAINTED SMILES

D.R. Mills

SEA OF INK PRESS

MONSTERS
PAINTED SMILES

Cover art: MiblArt
Interior book design: Enchanted Ink Publishing
Illustrations: Gabrielle Ragusi
Editing: A. P. Mobley at Sea of Ink Press

ISBN: 978-1-7358479-6-2 (Paperback)

SEA OF INK PRESS

For Crutches.

Thanks for being someone
I could always lean on.

D.R. MILLS
PRESENTS . . .

MONSTERS

PROLOGUE

JOHNNY JAMISON HAULED the heavy mahogany trunk up the old stone stairs, heading toward the front doors of Wellington Theater. Tears stung his eyes, blurred his vision, and his chest tightened with fresh, burning anger as he heaved the doors open and trudged inside.

He should have known it would come to this. He should have known something like this would happen. Now his children were gone, and they were never coming back.

Wellington Theater's main hall was dark, the familiar scent of stale air and popcorn making Johnny's stomach sick. More so than it already was, anyway. He walked across the long red-and-gold rug that ran through the pathways of the building. As he ascended the stairs just ahead of the entryway, the trunk he was dragging began to shake and shudder.

A nasty jerk nearly wrenched him back down a few steps. Heart pounding, he spared a hand from the box's handle and grabbed onto the railing, clasping it so tight he wondered if his grip would bend the metal.

Once Johnny regained his balance, he clenched his jaw, hardening his resolve, and climbed up the last several steps. *I just need to reach the dressing room*, he thought. If his goddamn partner didn't manage to pull him down the stairs, there wasn't much further to go. His room was only one more floor above him, on the theater's third level.

With the trunk in tow he plodded down another hall, along more red-and-gold rugs toward the next staircase. As always, he couldn't help but glance at the walls as he passed. They matched the carpet and were lined with photos of the incredibly talented people who had performed under Wellington's roof.

A few of the portraits featured Magician Gregory Vails, a smile permanently plastered on his round cheeks. Rachel and Hannah Glockner, twin sisters who could move their flexible bodies in unusual ways, also adorned the walls. Even Bill Haddorn had a picture up there, posed next to his prized dalmatian, Spot, who performed all manner of magnificent tricks on command.

Many of the people who had performed at Wellington Theater possessed skills that made them interesting, and then there was Johnny. His portraits in the hall were double the number of everyone else's combined, and wherever he looked, he saw his own face. But it was the face of a fraud. He didn't deserve to be up there at all.

Three years ago, Johnny had started performing at Wellington, and, according to the owners, he'd single-handedly saved the place from going bankrupt. The theater had still been nothing to sniff at, though. Even then it stood eleven stories high and housed an abundance of dressing rooms and backstage departments, and it also had a kitchen and recreation area for staff. Not to mention the fact that the auditorium could fit over half the town of Twilight Peak. In short, it was a monster of a building.

Almost there, he thought, tramping up the staircase to the third floor, lugging along the box that stored all of his problems. *If I can just...*

The trunk jerked again, the force nearly tugging him down once more. He glanced back at the hunk of wood, his fury and the tightness in his chest worsening as memories of the past few hours flooded back. "Stop it!" he screamed.

However, what he wanted didn't matter to the thing in the trunk. There was a giggle from beneath the latched lid. "Or what?" asked a shrill, masculine voice–Johnny's partner. "I already told you, Johnny Boy! You can't get rid of little ol' me so easily!" Hearing his partner's voice made Johnny's gut twist into knots. Honestly, it had always made him uneasy. After tonight, he hoped to never hear it again.

Johnny gave the trunk a sharp tug as he reached the top of the steps, then set it down to catch his breath. Hot tears welled in his eyes again, obscuring his vision, but he held them back, willing himself to stay strong. The nightmare was almost over. "I'm going to get rid of you," he said. "Even if it kills me."

Another chuckle sounded from inside the box, but this one was laced with malice. "We'll see."

Five minutes passed, and Johnny grabbed the trunk and continued down the hall. Finally, he arrived at his massive oak door. *Johnny L. Jamison* had been carved into a metal plate that hung above the entrance. He turned the knob and pushed it open, his arms burning. He was determined to finish this.

The room was well-organized, as it always had been, illuminated by the eerie white glow of the moonlight shining in from a bay window. Johnny could see his desk, his cabinets, his baskets full of props, and the closet that contained his entire on-stage wardrobe. The only thing he couldn't see was the portrait of himself and his partner, which hung on the far-left wall above his giant fireplace. The picture remained just out of light's reach.

He took a few deep breaths, trying to calm his nerves. After all, the binding spell he'd been given should keep the evil sealed forever. That's what he hoped, anyway.

Hands trembling, Johnny dropped the trunk and hurried to the portrait. He seized it and set it on the floor, then ran his fingers along his stone fireplace, memories of his first performance rushing back to him. *How naive I was*, he thought. *How desperate for success. If only I could go back.*

But he couldn't go back. All he could do was try to make things right.

He felt around, found the loose brick, and pulled on it. It slid out halfway, then stopped, the top half of the fireplace sliding upward. The grate tipped inward, becoming a "bridge" he could safely walk over. He hastened across the grate toward the vault door–a secret passage shrouded by stone.

Johnny stepped past the rock to find the combination lock keeping the vault secure, then dialed in the correct numbers and opened it with a soft *click*. He pushed open the door and stepped into the hidden portion of his room: a chamber made of steel, its only light source that of a battery-powered desk lamp. However, instead of storing more gear for his performances, this area overflowed with his research on the occult. There were papers strewn about the floor and stuck to the walls, maps with marked and crossed-off locations, and so much more he could not see in the dark.

Johnny swung around and ran back to the main dressing room. He grasped the trunk and began dragging it into the safe room. Once he got the box inside, he slid it across the floor, leaving it in the center of the mess.

"This isn't over, Johnny Boy," his partner shouted. "I can't stay trapped forever! Once I'm free, there'll be nothing you or Magnus can do to stop me!"

Johnny ignored these words. There was no way his partner was getting out of this room, let alone the trunk. In fact, the symbol painted on the inside of the door should seal everything inside once Johnny shut it. Nothing magical or otherwise could get in or out afterward.

It took Johnny a few minutes to gather his things from the steel chamber. He collected everything he might need later–jewelry, old relics, papers brimming with notes and knowledge. Soon there was nothing left except the desk, the lamp, and the trunk.

As Johnny turned to leave, his partner called to him one last time. "Your daughter screamed for you before I got her. You can't kill me, and you can't get her or the other brats back. Any way you slice it, *I win*."

Sudden searing rage erupted in Johnny's chest. He gritted his teeth, his whole body shaking. He balled his hands into fists. More than anything, he wanted to throw open that trunk, seize his partner by the neck, shred the thing until it was nothing but splinters…

No, he thought, and finally allowed the tears to leak from his eyes, to slip down his cheeks. *That won't do anyone any good.*

Conjuring his last bit of willpower, Johnny slammed the vault door shut. "Rot in hell you little monster!"

A loud *clang* sounded all around him, sealing away his partner's endless cackling, and he sank to the floor. Then he allowed himself to cry. Rip out fist-fuls of hair. Scream.

Johnny wept for hours, for his daughter and sons he couldn't save. For himself, for finally being free of this evil.

Still, his partner was right. Whatever angle he evaluated the situation from, Johnny had still lost.

CHAPTER ONE

TWENTY-EIGHT YEARS LATER...

CHYANN SAT CROSS-LEGGED on a couch in the Fleck family home, silently reading the novel nestled in her lap. The book was nothing special, just some old romance story. Not her usual reading material, but she needed to study it for an English assignment. Anything to keep her mind off of last week's events.

The bark of a dog and several pounding footsteps tore her from the page she was on, and she looked up to see Bobby, the ten-year-old boy she was babysitting, and Davey, Bobby's German shepherd. Bobby pivoted to face Davey and raised his arms toward the ceiling. "Boo!" he yelled in a playful tone. On cue, the dog spun around and began running from Bobby. The ten-year-old chased after him.

As Chyann watched Bobby and Davey play, the knots in her stomach began to ease. She'd always enjoyed babysitting the little boy, as he was well-mannered and had a big personality. The evenings she spent in the Fleck household were never dull, that was for sure.

Bobby glanced at Chyann as he chased his dog, then slowed to a stop and faced her. "Hey!" he shouted, pointing at her. "You're smiling!"

The statement seemed like an odd thing to get worked up over, but it struck Chyann upon hearing it. Honestly, she hadn't smiled since she'd arrived earlier in the night. Come to think of it, she hadn't smiled at all this past week–not since she'd faced her first-ever vengeful spirit.

"Yeah?" Chyann replied. "So what?"

"You've been really grumpy tonight," Bobby said. "I didn't think you'd smile at all."

She pursed her lips and set her book aside, then patted the cushion next to herself. Bobby scampered that way and launched himself onto the couch beside her, and she turned to face him. "I'm sorry I've been such a grump," she said.

"A mega-grump," Bobby agreed.

"Nuh-uh!"

"Yes-huh, you big sourpuss!"

Chyann couldn't help but laugh. "The point is," she continued, "I've had a lot on my mind lately. A bunch of stuff has happened, and it's bumming me out. That's all."

"What kind of stuff?" Bobby asked, sounding genuinely curious. However, it took Chyann several moments to identify *everything* that was upsetting her, considering there was so much. Horrible images flashed in her mind–the construction site and the crazy, gun-wielding man named Steve Helsing who'd taken her and her friends hostage. The cemetery, and how she'd had to dig up a corpse there and set the body ablaze. The house down the street and the ghost of Adella Williams terrorizing the new family living in it.

She pushed the memories away as best she could, the hair on the back of her neck standing on end. "Oh, y'know. Just... usual teenager stuff. You'll understand when you're older."

"Oh..." Bobby's face dropped in disappointment. Chyann was sure he'd heard identical answers to his questions like this many times, but what else was she supposed to tell him?

She heard the door opening in the next room, and Davey barked, while Bobby's eyes widened with excitement. "Daddy!" he exclaimed, leaping off the couch like he had springs for legs and sprinting for the house's entrance, Davey following suit. Chyann slid a scrap of paper between the pages of her novel to mark her place, returned the book to her bag, and started after Bobby and Davey.

Edward Fleck had always seemed like a strong

man, tall and wide, with a refined jaw and a few gray hairs popping up in his dark hair. He wore a bright-orange safety vest, the rest of his clothes covered with muck. Dirt stuck to his sweat-covered face, although the space around his eyes appeared clean enough, probably due to the goggles he always donned while doing construction at work.

Ed knelt and embraced Bobby, and Davey licked the man's hands. Chyann hugged her arms against her chest, standing nearby. It didn't take long for Ed to notice her. "Hey, Chy," he said, then released Bobby and stood.

"Hey," Chyann replied.

Ed's expression morphed into one of concern. "You okay? You look a little spooked."

"Yeah, I'm fine," she lied. "I've just been on edge lately."

"School weighing you down?"

Chyann snorted, forcing herself to smile. "Always."

Ed gave her a nod. "Well, hang in there. You can get through it."

"Thanks."

"She's been super sad all night long," Bobby chimed in, dashing back to the living room.

Ed removed his safety vest and hung it on a hook by the door. "Has he been this energetic all night?" he asked.

Chyann shook her head. "Only for the last hour. He ate all his dinner, so I gave him a brownie for dessert. If you're lucky, he'll be conked out in the next twenty minutes or so."

"If I'm lucky," Ed repeated with a laugh, walking past her. Chyann chuckled as well, then slipped on her shoes and returned to the living room.

As she grabbed her bag, Bobby hugged her legs from behind. "Bye, grumpy!"

Chyann cracked a smile and turned around to give him a proper embrace. "I promise I'll be happier tomorrow night, okay?"

"Pinkie swear?" He held a pinkie up.

Chyann wrapped one of her own little fingers around his. "I pinkie swear."

"If you break it, I'll never talk to you again," he said. "Those are the rules." And Chyann knew he was serious. Bobby joked about tons of stuff, but this wasn't their first pinkie promise, and he always meant it when he made them.

"I understand." She let go of his little finger and pointed at his shirt collar. "You've got some spaghetti on your shirt."

"Nuh-uh!" Despite his protest, he still looked down at his shirt, and Chyann poked his nose. "Hey!" he shouted, giggling, and pushed her hand away.

Chyann offered her best maniacal-cartoon-vil-lain laugh. "*Ha-ha-ha*! Gotcha. I'll see you tomorrow, all right?"

"All right." He gave her one more hug before hur-rying up the stairs.

With her bag in tow, Chyann headed for the front door. Ed opened it for her as she approached. "Thanks again. See you tomorrow night."

"Anytime. See you then." She stepped outside,

a cold gust chilling her and rattling the bushes and trees in the yard. It was already pretty dark, her only illumination that of the streetlights and the quarter moon overhead.

Chyann's chest tightened with anxiety, her breaths growing shallow. She opened her bag and reached inside to retrieve her Taser gun. Once she found it, the panic in her chest began to dissipate.

It was a standard-issue Taser, which once belonged to Chyann's mother before Mom's retirement from the force. It hadn't been difficult to steal or hide, either, considering Mom was hardly ever home. Not that keeping it a secret really mattered, anyway. If Chyann got caught with it, she was sure Mom would let her keep it for self-defense.

Chyann took a minute to steady her breathing, then stepped off the porch and around the railing toward her bike. She climbed on and began pedaling away, but she made sure to keep an eye out for anything suspicious. It was an easy ten-minute ride home, but she figured the trip would feel much longer than that.

CHYANN FUMBLED WITH her keys for a moment before managing to find the correct one, the porch light buzzing overhead. She unlocked the door and tiptoed inside, then shut it behind her and set her bag down. *Finally home*, she thought. *At least I feel safe here.*

She leaned against the door for a minute, its cool wood like ice on her skin. Her hands trembled, and she pressed her face into them, willing them to calm. They hadn't stopped shaking since she'd encountered Adella a week ago at Sadie's house.

She sighed deeply; the action felt like the only thing keeping her from breaking down. Tears pooled in the corners of her eyes, but she held them back with every fiber of her being. *You're okay, Chy. You're okay... Keep it together.*

There was a sharp *creak* farther into the house, and she shot her head up. *Was that a footstep?*

She listened intently, her blood running cold. A few seconds passed, but that was enough time for her to question herself. Was she just being paranoid?

Another *creak* sounded from the kitchen. She froze in place, chills racing up and down her back. Goose bumps prickled her arms. *Keep it together.*

She took another quivering breath and reached into her bag. Once she found the Taser gun she pulled it out, held it at the ready, and tentatively approached the kitchen. Her sneakers *squeak*ed against the hardwood floor–they must have gotten a bit wet from the moist grass of her yard. Finally, she poked her head through the kitchen doorway, her throat impossibly dry as she spoke. "H-h-hello?"

Chyann took a step onto the kitchen's glossy linoleum and snapped on the light switch with her free hand. Instantly the room became visible. Everything seemed normal, all the utensils stored in their proper places. But wait... No, something was wrong. She looked closer and soon realized the bread and several condiments were sitting on the island countertop. Not only that, but a dirty plate had been left in the sink. *Mom hasn't been home tonight. She would have told me. And I know I did the dishes before I went to the Flecks'.*

There was another *creak* to the right. She flinched, looking over. A breeze came in through the window, the curtains billowing, the frame whistling as wind pushed against it.

She let out a breath of relief, walked over to the window, and shut and locked it. *That's all it was,* she thought. *I just forgot to close the window before I left. Nothing to worry about.* She strode over to the counter and set the Taser down, then examined the bread and condiments. *I remember making a sandwich before I went over to babysit. Did I forget to shut the window* and *to put this stuff away?* She grabbed it all and headed for the cupboard.

As she was putting everything away, she caught a glimpse of her reflection in the glass, and her heart fell to her stomach. A dark shape stood behind her, arms raised as if ready to snatch her. "BOO!"

Chyann dropped the food and spun around. She seized the assailant's arm and bolted behind them. She slammed them face-first onto the counter and yanked their right arm behind their back. Then she put pressure on the limb, threatening to pop it out of the socket. "Ow, Chy! Take it easy!" the intruder cried.

Chyann stopped. She knew that voice. Her adrenaline was high, her pulse pounding like a drum in her ears, but she managed to let him go. "Will?"

Willy turned to face her as he rolled his shoulder. "Jeez! Don't wing me, huh? I need that arm."

"Don't scare me like that then, you asshole!" she yelled. "What the hell is wrong with you?"

"Hey, if I knew you were gonna pull one of my limbs off, I would've surprised you from over there."

Chyann punched him, tears clouding her vision. "Why would you do that?"

"Holy crap, calm down." Willy raised his hands in defense, chuckling. "It was just a joke!"

"Yeah?" She punched him again, this time with all her strength behind it. "Well, it wasn't funny. Do you have any idea how scared I was?"

"Well," Willy began, rubbing his arm, "considerin' how bad you prob'ly just bruised my arm, I'm gonna say pretty damn scared." He smiled, apparently oblivious to how serious the situation was.

She squeezed her fists so hard her nails dug into her palms. It drove her crazy when he acted like this. She wanted to tell him he was being insensitive. That he shouldn't have been in her house to begin with. That he had pissed her off beyond comprehension. However, all she could manage was a cry of indignation, and then she whirled around and started stomping away.

"Oh come on, Chy!" he said. "I'm sorry I scared you." But the apology wasn't genuine. She could hear that he was trying not to laugh. She grabbed her Taser and tramped into the living room. "What?" Willy continued, trailing after her. "Do I have to get on my hands and knees and beg?" Chyann refused to reply. Instead, she snatched up her bag and pounded up the stairs toward her bedroom, Willy still following her.

Once she reached the top of the staircase, she ran to her bedroom, slammed the door shut, and locked it before Willy could get to it. Releasing another frustrated sound, she threw her stuff onto her bed.

A soft knock sounded at the door. "Chy, come on. I was just messin," Willy said. "I didn't mean to scare you that bad." Sincerity laced his tone now, and it didn't seem like he was holding back laughter anymore, either. *I should still send him away*, a part of her thought. *After everything we've been through—Boss, Steve, Adella—what he just did was seriously messed up after all that.*

However, another part of her didn't want to send him away. She'd been so scared of being alone recently...

She turned around, unlocked the door, and opened it. Willy offered her a guilty smile. "Really, I'm sorry. That was dumb to do."

"Yeah, it was."

"What's with you lately? You've been actin' real weird."

"What? No I haven't," Chyann argued. Willy didn't seem convinced. She rubbed her eyes, a wave of exhaustion suddenly hitting her. "Really, I'm fine. I'm just tired. I've had a long day." Willy still didn't seem like he believed her, but he didn't press further, either. "What are you doing here this late, anyway?" she asked.

"Well," he began, his signature smirk returning, "my folks are screamin' so loud the cops can hear 'em before our neighbors even have the chance to call, so." He paused and pointed at her floor. "I, uh–I figured I'd come take my usual spot or somethin'. If that's cool?"

"Yeah, that's fine," she said, nodding. It wasn't abnormal for Willy to come stay at her place. In fact, it had become almost regular. Chyann didn't know his parents all that well, but she had heard one of their fights a few years ago. She didn't blame Willy for staying at either her or Ryan's house so often.

"Sweet," he said, and Chyann noticed how bloodshot his eyes were, how dark bags had formed beneath them. He hung his head and walked into her room, then plopped down onto one of her softer beanbag chairs next to the bay windows. "Yeah... super comfy."

Chyann retrieved her pajamas and a spare blanket from her dresser. She tossed the blanket to Willy, then headed for the bathroom connected to her room. Right before she closed the bathroom door, Willy whispered, "Hey, Chy?"

She turned back to him. It looked like he was already falling asleep. "Yeah?" she said.

"Thanks." At this, Chyann's chest warmed. Having Willy here had already made her feel more at ease, even if he was barely awake.

"Anytime, Will," she replied, and closed the door.

CHAPTER TWO

DUST STIRRED, FALLING ALL around Ed Fleck like snow as he pried the door open and pushed himself inside. His crewmates, Ron and Vic, followed him as he walked forward and admired the main hall. It was a big, open chamber, with red-and-gold rugs sprawled across the floor. Painted graffiti peppered the walls and furniture.

Ed sucked in a long breath. He had missed Wellington Theater; this place had been a big part of his childhood. As a kid, he'd attended countless shows here. Seeing the building in such disrepair made his chest tight, and it didn't help that he was currently searching the place for the best spots to place explosives. As he stepped farther inside, though, his head spun with happy memories, nostalgia taking over. *When I get home tonight, I'm gonna have to bust out some of my old tapes for Bobby to watch*, he thought.

Something bumped Ed's arm, and he turned to see Ron standing next to him. The man handed Ed a flashlight and another hard hat with safety glasses. "Close your mouth, Ed," Ron said. "You're drooling."

"Smart-ass," Ed replied with a laugh. He grabbed the hat and placed it on his head, then took the flashlight and continued forward. "You guys didn't grow up here. You don't understand how amazing this place was back in the day."

"It's definitely a nice building," Vic agreed as he turned on his flashlight. His beam cut through the dust-covered darkness to guide their way. "Puttin' it together must've been somethin'."

"Seeing it like this, though… it's weird," Ed said as they walked toward a staircase. "It sucks that it's so run-down, but at the same time"–he clicked on his flashlight as well and shined it around the room–"it's like a giant time capsule. Everything looks exactly how it used to, more or less."

"I'm sure," Ron replied. "Besides the graffiti, right?"

"Big abandoned building," Vic stated matter-of-factly. "Graffiti is to be expected."

Ed shined his light at the staircase to the left. "That's how you get to the stage. Let's check it last."

"Right, then?" Vic asked.

"Right," Ed said.

And so the three men wandered up the creaky stairs to the right, the wood groaning under their footsteps. It was as if the building itself ached from being uninhabited for so many years. When they reached the top of the steps, they weren't surprised to find the hallway there had been vandalized as well. Velvet was torn from the walls, portraits of the various performers at the theater missing or broken.

Ed recognized many of the faces in the pictures. A pair of flexible twin sisters who bent their bodies in ways most believed impossible. A magician named G. Vales. A man with a dalmatian, although Ed couldn't remember their names.

"Who are these guys?" Vic asked.

"Performers," Ed answered. "They're what sold the theater back in the day."

"They don't look like showstoppers to me," Ron said in a dull voice. "No offense."

"Trust me, they were entertaining," Ed replied.

Vic illuminated a picture on the floor near the end of the hall and ambled over to it. With a gloved hand, he plucked it up and examined its grime-covered surface. "What about this guy?" He raised the frame for Ed to see. It was heavily cracked, and what was left of the frame was held together by a single nail. Ed guessed troublemakers had thrown it from the wall and stomped on it. Regardless of its damage, Ed recognized the person it featured.

He pointed at the photo proudly. "That guy was the headliner for every show. Johnny Jamison."

"Lemme guess," Ron began, "he was a comedian."

Ed snapped his fingers. "You're only half right. He was also a ventriloquist." Ron rolled his eyes and turned away. "What?" Ed asked.

"Dummies are creepy, man," Ron said. "And that Johnny guy was probably super-popular with the little kids because they were his preferred crowd, if you know what I mean."

Ed grimaced. "He wasn't like that."

"Yeah, yeah, sure he wasn't." As Ron finished his sentence, the floor *creeeaaak*ed beneath him. There was a loud *snap*, and then Ron yelled, his right leg plunging through the wood. He slammed belly-first onto the floor, clawing at the boards to keep himself from falling into the level below.

Vic dropped the portrait, hurrying to help Ron. Ed rushed forward as well. They seized Ron's arms and hauled him out of the hole.

"Screw this death trap!" Ron screamed, shaking a fist in the air, and Ed leaned over to examine the cavity. Rot had set in, blotching through the wood with bright discoloration. The entire floor was a hazard. It could give out anywhere.

Vic patted Ron on the back. "We knew this could happen."

"We're just gonna have to watch our step," Ed said. "Let's hurry and finish going through the rest of the building so we can head back downstairs." With Vic's help, Ed hauled Ron to his feet, and the three men trekked up another short staircase.

The next hallway was wider than the one below, featuring doorways in place of photos of performers. There was even more graffiti here, more than what they'd seen in the last two levels combined. Ron gestured at the doors. "What are all these, Vic?"

Vic reached into his back pocket, pulled out his blueprints, and peered down at the pages. "These appear to be…" He trailed off, readjusting his flashlight. "The dressing rooms. Yup, that's it."

Ed gazed ahead at the rooms. Many of their doors had been disconnected from the hinges, ripped from the walls by vandals. However, the one at the end of the hall was still intact and hung slightly ajar. The words, *Child Murderer* had been spray-painted onto the wood in white. Ed stared hard at the door, at what had been written on it. Something about it called to him. Sure, he and his crewmates had to search all the rooms. That was part of their job. But that room… something about it was different. He couldn't quite decipher what that "something" was, though. All he knew was he wanted to start there.

"Ed, where're ya goin'?" Ron asked, and Ed turned around, realizing he had been walking toward the door as if in a trance. Ron ushered him back over. "We got lots of rooms to go through. Just hold your horses."

Ed shook his head. "If we don't start now, it'll take all afternoon to get things going, and we gotta have the demolition started in a week." He continued toward the door. Ron swore at him, but he brushed off the slew of cusswords, eyeing the message painted on the door's old oak. Licking his lips, he wiped off the dusty nameplate on the wooden surface. *Johnny L. Jamison* had been engraved in the metal with fancy lettering.

Ed's pulse quickened, a rhythmic thumping sounding in his ears. He shoved the door open with a loud *creak*.

The door hit the wall. Its hinges came loose, and it slanted awkwardly, wobbling a bit. Ultimately, though, it fell still.

Ed shined his flashlight around the room, his jaw dropping as he stepped through the doorway. More white paint had been sprayed all around in here. The curtains had been drawn shut and tied over the gigantic window, blocking the afternoon sun's rays. Across from the window there was a large stone fireplace, and a portrait of Johnny Jamison hung above it. In Johnny's lap sat a ventriloquist dummy, but its face had been x'd out. It looked like someone had sliced up the canvas with a sharp tool.

What chilled Ed, however, was that the words *The man of the hour!* had been written on the picture. And, someone had left another message in the center of the floor: *The Show Must Go On.*

Ed halted, suddenly shivering. His teeth began to chatter, his breath coming out in an icy mist. Had the temperature changed?

His crewmates stopped beside him. "What the hell?" Vic whispered, and Ed swallowed hard. Steeling his nerves, he headed toward the carved-up portrait. Something about it made him want to get a better look.

The closer he got to the picture, the colder the air became, goose bumps rising on his skin. Once he reached the canvas, he paused and craned his neck to inspect it. *I wish I could see the dummy's face*, he thought, but the portrait was so torn up he suspected that even if he pressed the little strips of dangling canvas back into place, there still wouldn't be a complete image.

He turned around to see Vic and Ron as they inspected other parts of the room. Vic pushed aside the curtain to peer outside, but the window was covered with so much muck it didn't even let sunlight in. Ron kicked around a few pieces of wood; they must have been part of a desk or something.

Ed resumed analyzing the picture of Johnny and the dummy and caught sight of a piece of small, gold-plated metal set against the bottom of the frame. He leaned in to read it. "Johnny Jamison and W–"

The portrait crashed down on Ed's helmet before he could finish reading the plate. He stumbled to the side, shot out a hand to catch himself, and grabbed onto a brick on the side of the fireplace. The canvas landed facedown on the floor, kicking up a hurricane of dust. "Jeez, Ed," Vic yelled. "We're supposed to go through everything *before* we start knockin' the place down."

"Sorry," Ed replied. However, that wasn't the end of things. The slab he was holding on to pulled free, threatening to send him falling. He cursed and steadied himself, catching the brick and grasping it tight so it wouldn't hit the floor. Once he'd regained his balance, he crammed the block back into its spot on the fireplace.

A clicking noise came from somewhere within the wall, and the fireplace began to vibrate. Ed's eyes went wide as the top half of the fireplace slid upward, mechanisms behind the bricks pulling it apart. Its rusted grate tipped backward. Soon the grate appeared to become a walkway of sorts.

Once the vibrating stopped, Ed realized the fireplace had become a doorway that led to a small second chamber blocked off by a steel wall. There was a rust-covered dial and handle to the left, which had been hidden by the bricks. Inside, cobwebs fell apart like balls of cotton being stretched and pulled, and Ed guessed this area of the room had not been disturbed in a very long while.

He rubbed his eyes. *Am I seeing things?* He'd heard of secret safes before, but this was like something out of a book or movie. He lowered his hands and blinked a few times. The scene before him still hadn't changed: It was a concealed area behind a fireplace, triggered because he'd been messing with that brick.

As he contemplated why a secret room would be here, he faced Vic and Ron. They hadn't moved from their previous positions, and they wore expressions filled with shock.

"Hey, Vic?" Ron started. "Is there anything about that in the prints?"

Vic pulled out the blueprints and looked them over. He stopped on one page and squinted down at it for what seemed like hours before he looked up at Ed and Ron again. "Not a damn thing," he said, and Ed turned back to the new doorway.

"Well, what do we do, then?" Ron asked. "Tell the foreman?"

"Let's open it and see what's inside," Ed suggested.

"We could get in big trouble for that," Vic countered. "We don't even know what's in there. Not to mention the floor is rotting. If we mess with it too much, it could fall down into the basement."

"You kidding me?" Ed scoffed. "A safe this big? It's gotta have a ton of wall support or it would've fallen before the building was abandoned."

Ron gave the safe a leery glance. "What if we find a bunch of dead kids' bodies and shit like that?"

"For the last time," Ed yelled, "Johnny Jamison wasn't a creep!"

"As far as you know," Ron argued. "You didn't even know this stupid secret room existed." Ed couldn't refute Ron's point, and he recalled the stories people had told about Johnny back in the day. About how Johnny had killed his own children. However, Ed didn't believe the rumors. He refused to.

He returned his attention to the hidden doorway, then stepped toward the safe.

Fear that Vic's prediction about the safe making the floor cave-in built at the back of Ed's mind as he wiped dust and cobwebs from the door's dial and handle. When he finished brushing the muck away, all worries vanished, though. Curiosity took over as he noticed a symbol carved into the steel above the dial. The markings were hard to make out due to all the rust, but once Ed shined his flashlight on it, he could see it was a triangle with a circle in the center. Had the symbol been relevant to Johnny? Had it meant something to him?

Ed examined the rust a bit closer. It appeared to have gotten so bad it was weakening the lock. *Easier for me to crack the door open, then,* he thought. After all, any clues regarding the lock's combination were probably long gone by now. He knelt before the door and reached for the hammer and pry bar at his belt.

"Come on, man. Stop," Vic pleaded. "I don't wanna lose my job."

Ed readied his tools. "If the building owners find out, we'll tell them it was all me, okay? I'll let them know you tried to stop me and I broke in there anyway." He inserted the end of his pry bar into the rusted steel beside the dial and struck it with his hammer. Bits of weakened steel dislocated upon the impact, flying into the darkness as he swung again. This time, the dial popped out slightly, and he put his hammer away and began the extraction manually. It took less than a minute to pull the dial out from the wall completely.

"Holy…" Ed murmured. "Guys, look at this." Ron and Vic leaned over to inspect what Ed was seeing. The inside of the door–behind the space where the dial had once been—was nothing but red-and-orange grime.

"Looks like the entire thing rusted," Vic said. Ed didn't reply. He just stood, grabbed the handle, and wrenched on it. Loud *craaaaaack*s sounded from behind the door, and soon it came loose, swinging open with only a bit of resistance. Ed tugged it the rest of the way, and Vic shined his light into the safe. The interior was about the size of a small room, its steel walls rusted and cracking. Pale cottony strands hung from the ceiling like vines in a jungle, obscuring the crewmates' views as they peered inside.

Ed squinted. All he could make out was a desk with a lamp in the corner. Other than that, the chamber looked empty. Slightly disappointed, he used his pry bar to begin pulling some webs down, but soon he caught sight of something else. At the far end of the room a tarnished box sat, sealed shut and abandoned. He started toward it. "Careful!" Ron shouted at him. "We don't know how sturdy this thing is."

Ed paused and contemplated his next move. After a few moments passed he decided the risk was worth it, and he took tentative steps toward the box. Each time he put a foot down, he expected to hear groans and squeaks. But there were none. Yes, the floor was sturdy enough for him to walk across. He strode over to the box.

Once he reached its side, he brushed the top clean with his glove. It was pretty big, about the size of a recliner. *It's a trunk of some sort*, he realized, and felt along the sides until he found a handle. He gripped it tight and began hauling the box back into the main section of the dressing room.

When he finished heaving the trunk out of the safe, he stared down at it alongside Ron and Vic with uncertainty. A large iron padlock had been fastened to the lid's latch, but it too was covered with grime, except this stuff was a deep shade of burgundy.

Ed jerked his head back at the safe. "Did you see all the rust on the walls in there?"

"Yes," Vic replied. "It's like it corroded from the inside out."

"How in the hell does that even happen?" Ron asked.

Vic crossed his arms. "It doesn't. That room had to have been flooded for a number of months."

Ed turned back to the trunk, his thoughts whirring like gears in a clock. What could be in the box? Had it been Johnny Jamison's?

A pit formed in Ed's stomach. Was Ron correct about Johnny? Had he been a twisted, abusive person? Maybe Ed *didn't* want to know what was inside this thing, considering whoever had hidden it had gone to great lengths to keep it from being found.

"Well?" Ron's voice yanked Ed from his thoughts. "You risked our asses to get that hunk of scrap," he continued, motioning at the trunk. "You gonna open the damn thing or what?"

"Y-yeah, hold on." Ed's eyes had started to burn from all the dust swirling around. He blinked hard, returning his pry bar to his belt and retrieving his hammer. He rammed the tool against the box's pad-lock, and that was all it took to break it, which didn't surprise him in the slightest. He set the hammer aside, pulled the lock's remains away, opened the trunk, and peered inside.

What he saw made his breath catch in his throat. Today was filled with surprise after surprise. "No way."

Ron peeked inside, then ran his hands through his hair and turned around. "Aw, great."

Ed reached into the box and pulled out the dummy inside. The little guy's skin was smooth; he looked to be carved from the finest wood, with purple irises, a big nose, and defined cheekbones splashed with freckles. He had light-brown hair made from a wig-like material, slicked back to match how well-dressed he was. He wore a pristine white suit accented with a bright-red bowtie, a matching rose clipped to his left chest pocket.

"Is that… what I think it is?" Vic asked.

"It's Johnny's dummy!" Ed exclaimed excitedly. "It's Woody!"

CHAPTER THREE

"IF I ROLL A seven, I win," Bobby shouted confidently. He couldn't sit still in his seat at the table because of how excited he was. Chyann was only three spaces behind him on the game board, though.

"Don't celebrate just yet," she said as she grabbed up the dice. Bobby held his breath. He didn't want her to win. After all, he was so close! He watched as she shook the dice in her hands and rolled them onto the table. He counted the four and one she got and looked at the spaces on the board. If he guessed right, Chyann would land on the *Go Back to the Start* space. He jumped up and down with a victory cry. Chyann shook her head, smiled, and moved her piece back to the beginning.

"That means I'm gonna win," he said.

"Unless you land on that space, too," Chyann pointed out, resting her head on her arm. He looked back down to the board. There was no way he'd land on it as well. He gulped loudly–just as the characters in his favorite show did when they were nervous. Then he took the dice in his hand and shook them hard. *Please be more than five...* He held them a little longer than normal before tossing them onto the table. They landed, revealing his numbers: three and three. That put Bobby past the *Go Back to the Start* space, and it also put him one space away from the finish line.

Bobby jumped higher than ever before. "Yes! I won!"

Chyann shushed him, but her smile told him it was all right to celebrate. "You did," she agreed, and began to clear the board.

Bobby gestured for her to stop what she was doing, intending to ask her if they could play the game once more. However, a familiar sound made him pause–the squeak of the front door swinging open. "Daddy's home!" Bobby ran toward the front door. As he rounded a corner of the living room, he saw his father dragging a big dirty box into the house. Even though Dad's work clothes were filthy, Bobby jumped onto him and hugged him tight.

"Hey, kiddo," Dad said in a tired voice, returning Bobby's embrace. "How were things today?"

"Great! I beat Chyann at *Race 2 the Finish*," Bobby told him quickly.

Dad laughed, shaking his head. "You're a force to be reckoned with, that's for sure." He patted Bobby on the shoulder.

Suddenly remembering the box, Bobby looked over and pointed at it. "What's that?"

"Oh, this?" Dad smiled as he rested a hand atop the box's lid. "I think you'll like it." Bobby jumped up and down at these words. *Today just gets better and better*, he thought.

Dad's attention shifted to something behind Bobby. Turning, Bobby saw that Chyann had finally made her way into the room.

"Lost *Race 2 the Finish*, huh?" Dad asked.

Chyann shrugged, a guilty smile on her lips. "Landed on the *Go Back to the Start* space," she explained. Bobby moved past Dad to examine the dirty box.

"It gets the best of us," Dad replied before turning to Bobby. "Don't touch, okay? The trunk is filthy. I'll clean it once I change." Bobby nodded to show he understood, but he still wanted to examine the large container before him. Layers of dust coated it; it was almost as if the thing had been designed that way. Metal plates had been pressed over the corners, giving it an old-fashioned look, and its wooden surface was smooth, only chipped and scratched lightly in some places.

After studying the trunk a bit more, Bobby's curiosity became too much for him to handle. "What's inside?" he asked. Chyann crossed her arms, leaning against the wall. Dad grinned as he left the room, heading toward the kitchen. The man returned a few seconds later with a towel in hand. He wiped his palms clean, then used the towel to unlock the latches on the front and lifted the lid. Bobby leaned over to look inside, his breath catching in his throat. "Wow!" he shouted, and Dad reached inside to pull out a little man for all to see. Dad sat the doll on his knee. Its head fell to the side before suddenly springing to life, and soon the figure's eyebrows were moving up and down as his eyes looked side to side.

"Say hi to the kids, Woody," Dad said to the dummy.

"*Great to be here,*" Woody "replied"; Dad was obviously the one speaking. "*With all these animals running around, we could open a zoo!*" Bobby giggled hysterically at the joke. He turned toward Chyann to laugh with her, but she didn't seem to find any of this funny.

Dad handed the doll to Bobby, and the boy carefully took him and looked him over. "He's so cool," Bobby said.

"When I was your age, I used to watch him perform with Johnny Jamison at Wellington Theater," Dad explained. "I found him in Jamison's old dressing room today before we started tearing the building down."

"This thing's been in that abandoned theater all these years?" Chyann asked.

"Looks that way."

Bobby ran his hands over Woody's hair. It was slicked back and fancy, colored a light golden brown.

Bobby's gaze fell to the dummy's deep-purple eyes. They had so much detail and seemed to go deeper than Bobby could see. He wrapped Woody in a big hug, turning back to Chyann and Dad. "Can I go play with him?" he asked.

Dad glanced up at the clock with an unsure expression. "I dunno, bud. It's pretty late. You've got school tomorrow."

"You still need to clean up your crayons and toys, too," Chyann added.

"*Nooo*," Bobby whined. "I wanna play with Woody now! Can't I stay up a little?"

"No," his father said sternly. "It's a school night. Go clean your messes and get ready for bed. You'll have time to play with Woody tomorrow."

Bobby hung his head, tightening his grip on the dummy's body. "Can he at least stay in my room tonight?" He buried his face in the doll's white suit.

His father let out a tired sigh before nodding a couple of times. "Sure."

The energy returned to Bobby's legs. He spun around and started hopping away, intending to take Woody to his room upstairs. On his way up, he heard Chyann shout goodbye.

Soon he arrived at his door and pushed it open. Davey raised his head from the floor nearby. "Hi, Davey!" Bobby skipped past the dog to a child-sized rocking chair by the foot of his bed and set the dummy on it. Woody slumped over in the seat, his arms hanging limply off the side. "I guess we'll play later, Woody," Bobby said sadly. "I think you're really gonna like it here, though." The doll's head fell to one side as if in silent response to the statement, and Bobby turned and left the bedroom. Dad was right. He would have plenty of time to play with Woody tomorrow night. He patted Davey on his way out, then walked across the hall to the bathroom. He jumped onto the cold plastic stool, which brought him to the mirror's level, and reached for his toothbrush.

As he squirted toothpaste onto the bristles, a yipe sounded from his bedroom. He nearly fell to the floor in surprise at the noise. He turned around just in time to see Davey hurry out from his bedroom and run downstairs. *Did something scare him?* That didn't seem right. Davey wasn't a mean dog, but he wasn't a big softy, either. Bobby stepped off the stool and leaned over to peer into his room, hoping to see what had spooked his dog.

Nothing looked out of place. Everything was fine. Woody still sat in the chair. Even Bobby's bed still... No, wait. Something *had* changed. The dummy remained in his seat, but his position was different. He sat upright, his head straight, his hands folded in his lap. His right leg was crossed over his left one, his light-brown leather shoes hanging from beneath his white pants.

Bobby slowly stepped into the bedroom, his eyes scanning the dummy for any other new details. "Woody?" The doll couldn't have moved on his own. That was dumb to even consider. Still...

Bobby stared into Woody's deep-purple eyes, searching for something, although he wasn't sure what. The endless black pupils looked empty. Bobby felt himself getting lost in their darkness.

Finally, Dad's voice rang from downstairs, snapping Bobby out of his trance. "Bobby! Hurry and pick up your stuff!"

"Coming," Bobby shouted back, still staring at Woody. *Maybe I set Woody down in a nicer way than I thought.* It wouldn't be the first time he'd confused himself over little things like this. He shrugged and returned to the bathroom. "Huh, weird."

It didn't take long for Bobby to finish brushing his teeth, and once he did he hurried downstairs. He gathered up his crayons and drawings from the day, then ran to his room with them. When he saw Woody had not moved since he'd left, he felt relieved. *Maybe I just don't remember it right*, he thought. He put his crayons where they belonged, threw on his pajamas, and flicked on his bedside night-light.

As he crawled into bed he yawned, glancing at Woody one last time. "Goodnight, Woody," he mumbled before rolling over, closing his eyes, and drifting off into a deep, dreamless sleep.

CHYANN BIKED DOWN the quiet late-night street. Her breathing remained steady but constantly threatened to speed up. At least she was nearly home now. She'd arrive and everything would be fine, just as it had been the past two nights after babysitting at the Flecks' house.

She'd already pedaled over Donkey Bridge, which was usually the scariest part of her route. The river below the bridge wasn't immensely threatening–not in that area, anyway. Farther downstream was where the water grew more rapid, full of piercing rocks as it coursed down the mountain. A short ways down there was a sharp drop that meant certain death for any unlucky wanderer who fell into the stream and couldn't get out. It always made her nervous going across Donkey Bridge, but it was part of the easiest and quickest path from her house to the Flecks'.

As she continued pedaling, she caught sight of an alleyway up ahead on the right, and her mind began dancing with visions of unearthly creatures leaping out from the shadows and grabbing her as she approached. *Don't be stupid*, she thought. *There's nothing lurking around. You're just scaring yourself.*

Despite her self-talk, Chyann couldn't help but speed up so she could escape the passage quickly, trying to excuse the irrational behavior all the while. *I just want to get home sooner.* However, deep down she knew that seeds of paranoia had planted themselves deep within her mind.

"There's nothing in there," she whispered to herself, over and over. "There's nothing in there. There's nothing in there." Somehow, saying the words out loud helped convince her they were true.

Just as she reached the alleyway, there was a loud *hisssss.* A black shape darted out of the darkness and into her bike path.

Chyann screamed, panic filling her body like lightning in a rainstorm. She jerked her bike to the side to avoid the assailant, but her front tire caught the curb at the wrong angle. The force stopped all her momentum and sent her careening over the handlebars.

She hit the sidewalk, landing hard on her shoulder. But before she had time to register the pain, the hissing sounded again. Adrenaline surged through her body. She leapt to her feet, whipped out her Taser gun, and trained the weapon on the shadow before her.

Chyann stopped, relaxing as she realized what the shadow was. *It's just a black cat.* The cat released a final hiss and took off at breakneck speed.

Chyann lowered the Taser and pinched the bridge of her nose, a whirlwind of emotions flooding through her. Tears sprang into the corners of her vision, fueled by both relief and terror. Suddenly she wanted to laugh as well as cry, but she couldn't. Like it or not, this wasn't the place. She needed to get home.

She started for her bike. Hot pain seared her shoulder, and she remembered falling onto the sidewalk just moments ago. *Great*, she thought. *I probably scraped myself all to hell.*

She returned the Taser to her bag, then leaned down to retrieve her bike and hauled it into an upright position. As she began walking her bike away, she couldn't help but groan, the pain in her shoulder becoming more intense. What had started as a dull burn had become a fierce, blazing throb.

A streetlight up ahead beckoned her, illuminating the wide brick wall below with a fluorescent purple glow. *I'll stop for a sec and take a look at how bad I hurt my shoulder*, she thought. *Hopefully it's not as messed up as it feels.*

Once she reached the light, she leaned her bike against the steel pole, removed her jacket, and lowered the collar of her shirt until she could see the area causing her so much discomfort. Just as she'd hoped, it didn't look nearly as unpleasant as it felt. There was some blood, yes, but not much. Nothing some cleaning and a bandage couldn't fix.

She lifted her collar into place and put her jacket back on, her gaze wandering to the brick wall before her. She hadn't noticed the graffiti before, probably because of its small size, but it had been painted in black on the red-and-orange brick. It was simple: a triangle with an overlapping eye in the center. Judging by how much the image had faded, Chyann knew it couldn't be recent. She guessed it had been drawn around a year or two ago. Tagging wasn't one of her pastimes, but from everything Willy had told her about it, she knew a symbol like this was usually a kind of signature.

But that can't be right... can it? She scanned the rest of the wall, but there were no other paintings. *Why would someone leave a signature and nothing else?* Her phone buzzed in her pocket, startling her from her thoughts. She pulled the phone free, tapped the screen, and shut off her bedtime alarm. *So much for going to sleep at a reasonable hour.*

She cast one final glance at the symbol before putting her phone away and hopping onto her bike. Her shoulder seared as she pedaled, but she muscled her way through it, her will to make it home more powerful than any amount of pain.

CHAPTER FOUR

A LOUD VOICE SHOUTED Bobby's name from somewhere outside his room. He jumped out from under his covers and sat upright.

The voice bellowed again. "Get down here, *now*!" Bobby's blood ran cold. The voice belonged to his dad. And judging by how Dad sounded, he must be very unhappy.

Bobby leapt out of bed, then raced down the stairs and into the living room. Dad stood with his arms crossed, his eyes filled with anger. Bobby rarely made his dad mad, and this was why. The look on Dad's face scared Bobby more than anything.

"W-w-what's wrong?" Bobby stammered. His dad motioned to the wall nearby, and Bobby turned to look at it. A drawing of the Fleck household and four stick figures had been scribbled on the wall in red crayon–two of the figures were inside the house and two were outside. The pair of stick figures inside were labeled *ME* and *WOODY*. Meanwhile, the two stick figures outside read *JACKASS* and *STUPID DOG*.

"Look at me, son." Dad's voice was serious, and Bobby wondered whether he'd be punished. He hadn't done this, of course, but it looked as if he had. The picture on the wall was identical to some of his other drawings, and one of his red crayons lay on the floor.

He swallowed hard and turned to face his dad. "Go upstairs and get a bucket of warm water and a sponge," Dad said. "This is to be cleaned up before you leave for school. Is that clear?"

"But–"

"Is that clear?" his father repeated, this time even more sternly, and what remained of Bobby's courage melted like butter in the hot sun.

Bobby lowered his head and slinked toward the stairs. "Yes, Daddy..."

As he went upstairs, disappointment and confusion racked his thoughts. He knew better than to draw on the wall. So how had this happened?

One thing was for sure. It was going to be a long day...

LUNCH PERIOD HAD finally rolled around, and Sadie was thankful for that. She had walked out of the house this morning without eating anything other than a slice of unbuttered toast. Now she had a hot meal on the tray in front of her, and she was in good company with her friends. It didn't get much better than this.

As she bit into her hamburger, Willy continued their conversation.

"Seriously, though," he said. "It's like I don't even try anymore."

"Really?" Sadie asked between chews.

Willy leaned back in his seat, cool as a cucumber. "Oh, yeah. I come in, sit down, make one smart-ass comment, and I'm off to detention!"

Sadie giggled in response. "You can't be serious." She turned to Ryan for confirmation.

"Oh, he's serious," Ryan said, nodding, and stuffed a spoonful of macaroni and cheese into his mouth.

Sadie couldn't help but laugh again. She had learned so much about Ryan, Chyann, and Willy in the short week since she'd met them. Willy had been the first out of the three she'd heard rumors about. Most of her classmates made him sound like an awful, violent person. Some even claimed he'd almost killed two students. However, Willy wasn't like that at all. He was funny and laid-back, pretty much the complete opposite of what everyone around school said.

"Sometimes I don't even have to say anything," Willy continued. "One day I got sent to Bullworth's office because I was smiling and wouldn't tell the teacher why."

"You were smiling because you put a fake rat in her desk drawer before she came in," Ryan pointed out.

Willy shook a fist, feigning anger. "I know, and I missed her freak-out 'cause she sent me outta class before she opened the drawer."

Ryan laughed. "It was a pretty legendary freak-out."

Sadie giggled alongside Ryan, recalling the rumors she'd heard about him as well. He was known as the "creep of the school," and most were convinced he was some kind of cultist or serial killer. But when she remembered how awkward he'd been when she'd met him, she knew none of it could be true. In fact, when she thought about how much he'd stumbled over his words when they'd first spoken, butterflies fluttered in her stomach. Ryan was pretty cute, especially when he got nervous around her.

"Oh, and don't even get me started on that day in Wilson's class," Willy said with a smirk. "Chy can tell you all about that one. Right, Chy?"

Everyone at the table turned to Chyann, but she didn't answer. She had a faraway look in her eyes as she stared off into space. Sadie couldn't be entirely sure, but it almost looked as though the other girl was sneering.

Sadie hadn't discovered any rumors about Chyann yet. The only thing she'd heard about the girl was that she was a suck-up to the teachers, and a few students suggested she might be part of the "cult" Ryan supposedly belonged to. Unlike Ryan and Willy, however, most kids spoke pretty positively about Chyann. According to them, she was dedicated, smart, and a wonder to watch on stage during school performances. And, so far, Sadie found all those things to be true.

"Chy!" Willy yelled.

He seemed to have snapped her out of her trance. "Yeah?"

"Welcome back to Earth, space cadet," he said with a laugh.

"You okay?" Sadie asked Chyann. "You look a little pale."

"Yeah, I'm great," Chyann answered casually. "Just trying to review some things in my head. I have a test next class." Sadie only nodded in response. Chyann's answer didn't seem out of place, but there was something in her voice—unease, Sadie realized. She wasn't sure why, but she didn't believe a word Chyann had just said.

"Did ya hear what I was sayin'?" Willy said.

Chyann shook her head, her voice quiet as she spoke. "No, I didn't. Sorry." She still seemed distracted, her gaze shifting toward the table behind Sadie.

"I was tellin' Sadie about that prank I pulled in Wilson's–"

Before Willy could finish explaining, a burly hand slammed down in front of Sadie, and she flinched. She looked up to see Todd Hallow, his face twisted in a menacing expression as he loomed over all of them.

"What the hell?" Ryan shouted, and Todd swiped their trays of food off the table. The trays clattered to the floor, hamburgers and side dishes scattering about. All the while, Todd's eyes remained fixed on one person at the table: Chyann.

Todd raised a finger and pointed it at Chyann's face. "You know what? I'm sick of you acting so tough, Ponytail." Chyann returned Todd's glare, and he continued, "All you do is talk big when I put one of your buddies on the chopping block. You've thrown yourself between me and the creep one too many times."

Sadie motioned for Todd to calm down. "Todd, please–"

"*Shut up!*" he interrupted, and she flinched again. The entire cafeteria had gone quiet, all other conversations brought to a halt. Todd glowered at Sadie for another few seconds before turning back to Chyann. "Do you think just because you're a girl, I won't hit you?" he asked, and Sadie's skin pimpled with gooseflesh. There was an intensity in Todd's eyes that made her nervous. She had seen him angry before–when she'd dumped her breakfast on his head and stormed off. This was different, though. This was pure, unadulterated hate.

Willy stood, his chair screeching against the floor. "You trashed my food, and now you're threatening my best friend? You must be as dumb as you are tall." The back of Sadie's neck tingled. This situation was getting out of control.

"Hit me, Todd," Chyann challenged. "If you hate me so much, just do it already."

Sadie's eyes went wide. She couldn't believe what she was hearing, and apparently no one else could, either. Everyone at the table watched Chyann in surprise.

After what felt like years of silence, Todd spoke. "What?"

"You heard me," Chyann replied, her tone ice-cold. She climbed to her feet. "If you're so big and bad, then hit me."

At first, Todd looked as if he wasn't sure whether Chyann was serious, and then he smirked, sauntering forward and throwing a giant punch in her direction.

Before Sadie could blink, Chyann ducked beneath Todd's fist and zipped behind him. She hooked one arm around his and yanked it back. With her other hand she jerked his head backward as well, popping his chest out. Then she kicked out one of his knees. As he fell, she slammed his skull into the side of the table. He toppled to the floor in a heap. Sadie's jaw dropped. *No way did Chy just do that*, she thought.

Chyann paused for a moment before she knelt down next to Todd and punched him hard in the face. Then again, and again, and again. Todd covered his head with his arms as best he could. *Stop. This has to stop.*

Sadie jumped out of her chair and hurried to Chyann's side. She grabbed the other girl's arm and pulled her away from Todd. "Chyann, stop it!" she shouted.

Chyann appeared to be in a trance induced by rage. Sadie gave the girl's arm a gentle shake, and Chyann blinked a few times, as if she'd just awoken from a disturbing dream. Sadie grabbed her by the shoulders and offered a reassuring look. "It's over," Sadie said. "Todd's done."

Sadie turned to look down at Todd, and Chyann did the same. He lay on the floor, peeking up at them from behind his bruised arms. His expression was a mixture of fear and bewilderment, and his eyebrow had been split open. Sadie guessed the injury had occurred when he'd hit the table. *I'll bet he's just as shocked by Chyann as I am*, she thought.

She turned back to Chyann, but the other girl's stare remained fixed on Todd. Chyann stood for almost a minute longer before her eyes began glistening under the lights. Without another word she swung around, breaking Sadie's grip on her shoulders, and sprinted away. She bolted past students, tables, and even an approaching teacher until she reached the exit and disappeared.

It didn't take long for principal Bullworth to arrive alongside the teacher who had come to assess the situation. Sadie hadn't spoken to the principal much, and she didn't recognize the other guy, but she knew fighting on school grounds was a big offense.

"Hope you like detention, Hallow," the teacher she didn't know said. He and Bullworth helped Todd to stand, then carted the bully away.

Conversation among the lunch room slowly resumed as Sadie watched Todd and the teachers leave, and someone whistled from behind her. She turned around to face Ryan and Willy.

Willy plopped down in his chair, whistling again as he glanced around. "Well, that was… intense."

"Yeah, it was," Ryan agreed, squirming as he took his seat.

"Chyann seems off to me," Sadie began, "but maybe I'm wrong. You guys have known her longer."

"Oh, yeah," Willy replied. "She's definitely been weird lately." As Willy spoke, he bent over to retrieve his sandwich from the floor. "She keeps tellin' us she's fine, though."

"Well, she's clearly *not* fine," Ryan stated as Willy adjusted the contents of his sandwich and bit into it. Sadie scrunched up her nose in disgust, and Ryan did the same.

Willy chewed a few times before offering them a shrug. "Still good," he said, and Ryan shook his head.

Sadie faced Ryan. "I'll go find her, okay?" He gave her a nod and a smile, and she turned and walked away, her heart skipping as she did. Something about Ryan's smile seemed to do that to her. She had to admit, though, both Ryan and Willy were as clueless as you would expect teenage boys to be.

SADIE HAD SEARCHED the halls for only a few moments before she stumbled upon the girls' restroom. Honestly, she wasn't sure where else to look for Chyann. Sure enough, she heard dull sobs as she opened the bathroom door. At the sounds she felt slight relief; after all, she didn't want to risk getting lost in the still-unfamiliar school. However, she didn't want to hear Chyann crying so badly, either.

"Chyann?" she asked, following the cries to the stall at the far end of the restroom. The door was shut and locked, but Sadie approached, resting her palms against the cool metal. "Are you okay?"

Chyann whimpered on the other side. "Not really. I don't know what's wrong. I just... I don't know."

Sadie thought about the events leading to this moment, carefully constructing what to say next. "Does it... does it maybe have something to do with the ghost?"

More sniffling and stifled cries. "I... I think so. All those awful things I read about Adella, the things I saw, the things I did..." She paused, taking a few deep breaths. "It brought back a lot of memories. Things I haven't thought about in a very long time." Her voice trembled, and Sadie's chest ached for her. Chyann continued, "My older sister was getting involved with this same kind of stuff–the supernatural, I mean–before..."

Chyann didn't finish her sentence. Still, the comment caught Sadie off guard. "I didn't know you have an older sister."

"Most people don't." Chyann suddenly sounded flat, her voice no longer shaking so much. It seemed as if she was calming down. Sadie opened her mouth to reply but stopped. What should she say? Thankfully, before she had to come up with something, Chyann blew her nose and explained. "My sister, she–she went missing a long time ago."

Now Sadie *really* didn't know how to respond. Even offering her sympathies didn't seem like an effective answer. Chyann seemed so... well, normal, to Sadie. Sadie assumed Chyann was "ordinary" at least, considering the way she carried herself and how intelligent and successful she seemed to be. For all of those reasons, Sadie thought Chyann's home-life would be averagely healthy. *I can't imagine what a traumatic event like that would do to my family.*

"How are you doing it?" Chyann asked.

Sadie wasn't quite sure what Chyann meant by that. "What?"

"You've been acting so normal since Adella," Chyann said, and Sadie detected a hint of admiration in her voice. "It's almost like it never happened to you. All the while, I've been a mess. Paranoid, on edge. I even hit Todd..." She spat out that last detail, as if beating down Todd was a deplorable act. "I just wanted to keep hitting him until he was gone. But that's not me. It's not."

Sadie lowered her head, glancing down at the white-and-black checkered-tile floor. Despite what Chyann might think, she wasn't handling the aftermath of Adella any better. Since they'd defeated the vengeful spirit, she'd had countless nightmares, and the slightest creaks in the house had sent her mind reeling. Jaci hadn't been getting much rest, either. She had spent several nights sleeping in Sadie's room because she was too scared to stay in her own.

When Sadie really started to think about it, the only time she'd felt relatively at ease was here at school, surrounded by her new friends. The ones who had saved hers and Jaci's lives.

"I'm not dealing with it as well as you think I am," Sadie admitted. "In fact, Jaci and I have both lost sleep over it. We were left home alone the other night, and we went to the movies just so we wouldn't be in the house." She forced a laugh. Tears collected in the corners of her eyes. "Truth be told, I thought *you* were the one who was keeping it together after what happened."

Now it was Chyann who forcibly chuckled, and Sadie couldn't help but smile a bit. The situation was actually kind of funny–in a messed up, traumatic sort of way. "You, Willy, and Ryan have been helping me cope," Sadie continued. "The only time I can really forget about what happened is when I'm with you three."

"Why? We were the ones involved. I'm surprised you even wanted to keep hanging out with us afterward."

"You guys saved my life. Jaci's, too." Images from that night began flashing through Sadie's mind, ones she had been trying to push down. "Ryan and Willy risked their lives to protect us, and in the end, you saved the day. I was terrified the whole time, sure, but still, you three... you three were the most amazing 'team' I've ever seen. I wouldn't have been able to escape Adella myself, let alone come close to beating her." She paused, giving Chyann time to respond, but the other girl stayed silent. "My sister and I would have died in that house if it weren't for Ryan, Willy, and you, Chyann."

Moments of quiet passed before Sadie heard movement from inside the stall. The door opened, and Chyann stepped out. Her cheeks were flushed, the bathroom lights making the tear-soaked flesh beneath her eyes shiny, and Sadie still couldn't believe calm, collected Chyann had been reduced to such a state. However, Sadie figured that, considering how much her own tears were obscuring her vision, she didn't look much better.

Saying nothing, Chyann stumbled forward and wrapped Sadie in a tight embrace. Instinctively, Sadie hugged Chyann back.

Sadie wasn't sure how long they held one another in comfort, but it wasn't until the bell rang that Chyann mumbled into Sadie's shoulder, "Thank you."

"No problem."

CHAPTER FIVE

THE FLECKS' HOUSE WAS quiet tonight, but Chyann didn't mind. The rest of the school day after her talk with Sadie in the girls' restroom had felt… off. She'd caught many students watching her with strange expressions as she'd walked through the halls. Gossip had already begun to spread like wildfire. The more things changed, the more they stayed the same, she supposed.

She had to admit she'd been relieved when she'd arrived an hour ago at the Flecks' house, though. She'd discovered Bobby was grounded from a majority of his usual activities. It wasn't abnormal for the little boy to be in trouble–at least not any more than it was for other kids his age to be. And every time Chyann babysat Bobby when he was grounded, it meant her evening would be a relaxing one. *After today*, she thought, *that's exactly what I need. To relax.*

The only activity Bobby was allowed to engage in was watching TV, which was precisely the plan once he finished his dinner. Of course, Bobby had conveniently forgotten to mention he was grounded when Chyann had walked him home from school, but Ed had left a note to verify what the boy was and wasn't allowed to do throughout the night. The details of his crimes, however, were not included in the note.

"So, let me get this straight," Chyann began, dumping the remainder of the mac and cheese into her bowl on the counter. "You're grounded for drawing a bad picture on the wall, but you didn't actually draw the picture?"

"Exactly!" Bobby cried, exasperated. The ten-year-old had been arguing his innocence since Chyann had seen the note from Ed. There wasn't much of a drawing left on the wall, though, and Bobby had said that was because he'd had to clean it before school this morning.

"All right, well, say you didn't draw the picture. Who did?"

"I dunno," Bobby replied with a mouthful of macaroni. He was already halfway done with his bowl by the time Chyann finished filling her own. She sat down across from him at the table. "But now I can't have my crayons or my games, and I can't play with Woody."

He sighed sadly as he turned and looked to the left. Chyann followed his gaze. The dummy named Woody sat in a chair in the living room, staring forward with his blank purple eyes. And what Bobby said was true; the note Ed had left for Chyann was clear that Bobby was not allowed to play with the doll. That statement had been underlined and bolded, which made it more than just a rule. As far as Chyann was concerned, it was law.

Chyann pursed her lips. "Sorry, bud," she said, and started eating. She wasn't quite sure what else to tell the ten-year-old, and apparently he didn't have anything to add. They ate the rest of their food in silence before migrating to the living room.

As Bobby slid a DVD into the media player, Chyann curled up on the couch with her newest book in hand. It was a mystery story–something she preferred over the romance novel she'd been reading for class. Davey trotted into the room and curled up on the other end of the couch near her feet. Despite the noise of the movie, she managed to read a little over half of her book before deciding to put it down.

The second the credits started rolling, Bobby ejected the disc and selected his next watch. As he got another film ready, Chyann couldn't help but glance over at Woody. The dummy sat beside a shelf of DVDs, and although Bobby cast him sad looks, the boy left him alone. *Bobby's not gonna touch that old thing*, she thought. *He knows how much trouble he'll be in if he does.*

As she looked at the doll more, the back of her neck began to prickle. It appeared as though his eyes had moved slightly. That he was staring back at her. She couldn't explain it, but it seemed as though there were... well, malice in his expression. But no, that couldn't be. He was just a hunk of wood.

Chyann pushed the silly thoughts from her mind and opened her novel back up. She was being ridiculous. Dummies were creepy, and that's all it was. Even so, she felt as if the doll were staring at her as she read, and it was getting harder and harder to fall back into the story, so she set the book down once again.

"Hey, Bobby," she said. "Since you're over there, can you do me a favor?" Bobby turned to look at her, and she pointed at Woody. "Can you turn his head the other way so he's looking at something besides me?"

Bobby leaned over and moved Woody's head to the side so it was facing the television. "It's rude to stare, Woody."

Chyann's neck stopped prickling, the unease lifting from her like a blanket being tugged away. "Thanks, bud." Now she could get back into her story. She scanned the page for where she'd left off. Once she located it, though, she only managed to read a handful of words before Bobby started yelling.

"Hey!" the boy exclaimed.

Chyann looked up to see the ten-year-old inspecting Woody's hands. "What?" she asked.

Bobby leapt to his feet and took a step back from the dummy. "*It was Woody!*" His shout was so loud it woke Davey. Startled, the dog scurried into the next room.

"What?" Chyann asked again, louder this time.

Bobby faced her, pointing at the doll. "The drawing. *I told you it wasn't me!*"

She knit her brow. Was Bobby seriously suggesting that Woody had drawn on the wall? "Bobby–"

"He has crayon on his hands, Chy!" Bobby interrupted. "*Red crayon!* Just like what was on the wall this morning. See, *look!*"

"Okay, okay, calm down. Use your inside voice." Chyann bookmarked her page and set her novel aside. She climbed up from the couch and walked hesitantly over to Woody, unease rising in her throat. Ignoring the feeling, she grabbed one of the dummy's hands and lifted it up to discover that Bobby was right. Bright-red smudges stained the inside of Woody's fingers and the edges of his palm. Even beneath the dim lamplight, Chyann could confirm the stains had come from crayon.

She shook her head. What exactly did this prove? That the dummy had drawn on the wall instead of Bobby? But that was silly, wasn't it? In fact, it simply wasn't possible.

"See? I was telling the truth," Bobby stated proudly, although he hadn't convinced Chyann. She knew it was out of character for him to draw where he wasn't supposed to, but that didn't mean it made sense for the doll to have committed the crime. "You believe me, don't you?" he asked.

She faced him. He looked desperate for an answer. "I…" She trailed off. *Am I really supposed to humor the idea that a dummy did this rather than Bobby?* Her stomach sank. The situation felt off, sure, but she had to force all unrealistic notions away. "I don't know," she finally answered.

"But I'm telling the truth!" Bobby screeched.

Before the conversation could escalate, Chyann heard the front door open. "I'm home!" Ed called, his boots clunking on the floor.

Bobby's eyes grew wide. "Daddy!" He wrapped his arms around Woody and lifted the dummy up and away as he hurried toward the front door. "Daddy, I know who did it!"

Chyann followed Bobby around the corner to find Ed in the entryway. He was covered in dirt and grime, as per usual. However, his eyes and the area around them were clean, protected by the safety glasses he had removed. "Huh?" Ed said. "Did what?"

Bobby lifted Woody's hands so Ed could see. "The crayon on the wall! It was Woody, see? He has red crayon on his hands."

The smile faded from Ed's face, his lips tightening into a deep frown as he knelt down to examine the doll. After some inspection, Ed took Woody away from his son. "Bobby, this is unacceptable," he said.

"What?" Bobby cried, visibly confused.

"This dummy is very old and valuable. If you can't take care of him, you can't play with him."

"But it wasn't me! Why doesn't anyone believe me?" Bobby ran down the hall and up the stairs to his room. He slammed his door shut, and Chyann turned to Ed. He trudged past her toward the closet.

"Sorry I'm late," he apologized, opening the closet door.

"It's fine. Besides, I'm all caught up on my homework."

Ed pulled out the trunk Woody had arrived in and slid it across the floor, then unlatched it and swung the lid open. "Well, thanks for staying late, anyway."

"Of course," Chyann replied. She headed back toward the living room to begin gathering her things. As she passed Ed, she saw him trying to scrape away Woody's crayon smudges with his fingernails, and the dummy's head was turned in her direction. She only caught a brief glimpse of his deep-purple irises, but the sight of them sent a shiver down her spine.

"See you tomorrow?" Ed asked.

She opened the front door. "Same time as always." Ed gave her a smile before gently placing Woody inside the trunk.

As Chyann closed the door and stepped outside, the pit in her stomach returned. She sighed. The fear just kept coming back. Refused to stay buried.

Maybe something wasn't right.

No, I'm being paranoid, she thought, *because of Ryan and Boss, and because my hometown is supposedly "cursed."*

When she really started to think about it, the notion of Twilight Peak being cursed sounded ridiculous. Yet here she was, walking down the dark red-brick sidewalk toward her house, nervously glancing back at the Fleck place.

Her hands began shaking. She slid one into her shoulder bag to grab her Taser gun. However, whole seconds passed and she still couldn't find it. She raised the bag and lifted the flap to peer inside.

Her stomach sank even more than before; the Taser was gone. Had she forgotten it at home, or had she left it at the Fleck household?

Not wanting to bother Ed, she decided to simply quicken her pace and brave the rest of the journey without it. *If it's not at the house, I can check the Flecks' tomorrow when I'm there.*

ED STEPPED OUT of the bathroom, running a towel over his buzzed black hair, the steam from behind soothing his sore, tired muscles. He always looked forward to a hot shower after a long day, and once he finished drying himself off, it was time for bed.

He strolled down the hallway, wrapping the towel over his shoulder and tightening the strings of his pajama pants. Once he reached Bobby's bedroom door, he stopped and cracked it open. The lights were off, Bobby's room illuminated only by the orange night-light in the corner by his bed. Thankfully, Bobby was fast asleep, one of his legs stretched out off the side of the mattress.

Ed couldn't help but smile. Bobby had always slept in odd positions. Ed hoped it was something his baby boy would never grow out of.

Ed made sure Davey was snoozing peacefully at the foot of Bobby's bed, then closed the door as quietly as possible and headed down the hall toward his own room, mulling over the day's events. *Although I hope Bobby doesn't grow out of sleeping funny*, he thought, *I pray he* does *grow out of drawing on walls.*

Ed had been more than surprised to find the red scribbles on the wall this morning, considering Bobby hadn't done anything like that since he was five years old. Ed had figured Bobby knew better, but apparently he'd been wrong.

Ed switched off the hall light and walked into his bedroom. The trunk containing Woody sat against the wall next to his sliding closet doors, but he hardly cared about the dummy right now. Sleep beckoned him, and he suddenly realized his eyes were growing heavy. He climbed into bed, the coolness of the crisp sheets melting away the last of his aches and pains.

Ed felt as if he had fallen into a cloud, and the second his head hit the pillow, he started to drift off, the only sounds that of the house settling. A *creak*. A laugh. A few *tap tap tap*s from the window blinds…

Wait a minute.

He opened his eyes and listened for more unusual noises, but there was only silence. Had he dreamed of the laughing? The tapping?

Another laugh echoed from the hallway. Ed shot up in bed. He threw off his covers, swung his legs over the mattress, and started tiptoeing toward the hall. The hardwood floor felt cold on his bare feet.

There was another laugh. Then more noises Ed couldn't decipher. Although the sounds were faint, they were loud enough that he thought they could be coming from either the living room or the kitchen.

He crept down the stairs. When he reached the bottom, he noticed a dull white glow coming from the living room. He could also hear voices, though he couldn't make out what they were saying. Ed's heart began pounding so hard, he wondered if a baby alien would burst from his chest like in those old sci-fi/horror movies.

Another laugh. No, it wasn't just one laugh–it was hundreds coming from an *entire crowd*. Ed risked a peek around the corner, and relief flooded him instantly.

The television was on, playing one of his old re-run VHS tapes of Johnny Jamison performing with Woody. Ed had fallen asleep watching it on the couch the night before.

Johnny had Woody sitting in his lap. The man politely asked the doll to be kind to the audience. "*Nuts to that!*" Woody responded, and a chorus of chuckles echoed off-screen. Ed stifled his own chuckle.

Did I leave the TV on? he wondered. *No, that's not right. Maybe Davey stepped on the remote and accidentally hit the play button before going up to Bobby's room.*

Ed shook his head. *Doesn't matter. Need to head back to bed.* He walked over to the entertainment center and clicked off the power on both the TV and the VHS player. Mystery solved. Now he could return to bed. It was pretty late, and he'd already lost his shot at a full eight hours of sleep. He retraced his steps out of the living room, but before he reached the stairs, a new noise–this one coming from the kitchen–caught his attention.

This sound was harder to recognize. If Ed didn't know any better… No, no. It couldn't be *that.*

He stepped into the kitchen, scanning his surroundings as best he could, his only light source that of the moon shining in from the window. It didn't take long for him to notice the sink was on. Water spurted out from it, overflowing and burbling across the linoleum floor.

Ed hurried toward the sink. *Dammit! Did Chyann leave the faucet on or something?* Feet and pajama bottoms soaked, Ed stepped past the table, turned both sides of the faucet off, and pulled the drain stoppers free.

His eyes practically burned with exhaustion, and now his chest practically burned with fury. It was going to take hours to clean this mess up, and that meant he'd lose even more sleep before going back to the construction site tomorrow morning.

Ed looked down to see the water was nearly ankle-deep. *Definitely gonna have to get a new floor. Of all the nights…* Light reflected off the water, casting ripples of luminosity across the room. The sight reminded Ed of his last job; he'd been a lifeguard at the city pool. He recalled the way the pool water had sent illuminations shimmering across the ceiling even after he'd turned off the lights for closing time.

As he turned to leave the kitchen, thinking of what to grab so he could get this mess into a more manageable state, he halted and stared forward, spotting something strange. All at once, a dozen new questions began swarming his thoughts. *What the hell am I looking at, exactly?*

Squinting, he realized he was looking at a small figure standing atop the island counter in the center of the kitchen. At first Ed thought the figure was Bobby, but then he realized it was too short to be Bobby.

Brilliant reflective ripples danced across the figure, and it was only because of them that Ed realized who stood before him: Woody the dummy.

Ed blinked hard. He rubbed his wet palms across his eyes. *Am I seeing things?* he wondered, but no, he wasn't. The doll was still on the countertop. "W-what–"

"Shocking, isn't it?" Woody interrupted. His voice was high-pitched, and it sounded just as Ed remembered, but more sinister.

Ed's head felt light. The room started to spin. Not only was Woody standing by himself, but he was also speaking by himself. *I have to be dreaming, right? That's the only explanation.*

As Ed continued wrestling with his perception of reality, Woody raised the hand he'd been hiding behind his back. In it he held... some kind of banana?

No, that wasn't it. The thing was yellow for sure, but it was less fruit-shaped and more like... *A gun*, Ed realized. *It's a Taser gun.*

"But not as shocking as *this*," Woody hissed, firing both prongs from the Taser. One hit Ed in the chest, the second in the neck, and searing pain overcame his senses. Suddenly agony was all he knew, all he felt. The world around him faded, and the only things he could process were the electricity jolting through his body and the malicious giggles coming from Woody.

The pain seemed to be never-ending, but still Ed fought against it, trying to remove the wires from his body. However, his arms wouldn't cooperate. They tightened and untightened against his will. His legs wobbled. He tried to step away, but he slipped in the water and tumbled. The last thing he saw was the side of the table. Then everything went dark.

CHAPTER SIX

RYAN AND WILLY HURRIED down a long white hallway, passing nurses and other hospital staff. Earlier that morning, Ryan had met with Willy at Larry's for breakfast like they did every Saturday. Chyann had been a no-show, and after waiting for her for an hour, Ryan and Willy had called her.

Now they were at the Twilight Peak General Hospital searching for room 415. A nurse had told them that's where they could find Chyann. Up ahead, Ryan saw where the hall forked left and right. The nurse had told them to go right when they reached it.

As Ryan went right, Willy went left. Ryan paused and swung around. "Dude!" he called. "She said to take the right."

Willy turned. "Yeah, she meant to take *her* right." Ryan crossed his arms, waiting for Willy to realize he'd misunderstood.

Willy didn't seem to get it, so Ryan continued, "Why would she have told us to take *her* right?" Willy still stood tall, but Ryan could see the gears finally beginning to turn.

Finally, Willy's smile faded, and he walked toward Ryan. "All right, you got a point." Ryan turned around and headed down the hall, shaking his head. It wasn't like Will to be so scatterbrained. Well, actually it was, but not as much as he had been since they'd left the diner this morning. In fact, as they'd neared the hospital, he'd almost stepped out into traffic. *He must be worried about Chy*, Ryan thought. *That's usually the only time he's this out of it.*

"What does he have to be worried about?" Boss asked from inside Ryan's head. *"Chyann is fine. Is she not?"*

"That's Willy for you," Ryan replied. The next corner they rounded led them to a relieving sight. Chyann stood in the hallway, espresso in hand as she stood by a window that looked into a patient room. "Chy, hey!" Ryan hollered as he and Willy ran toward her.

"You good?" Willy asked, and she turned to greet them with a tired smile.

She sighed. "I guess." She turned back to the window, and Ryan looked in as well. There was a little boy sitting in the patient room, and he was playing with some wooden blocks. Next to him sat a… ventriloquist dummy? One in a white suit. *That's weird*, Ryan thought. An unconscious man lay in a bed near the boy and the doll. Machines were hooked up to the man, fresh bandages wrapped around his head.

"What's the news?" Ryan whispered.

"Could be better," Chyann whispered back. "Ed's got some muscle damage from being seriously electrocuted, and he took a bad blow to the head. Otherwise, they think he's fine, but he hasn't woken up since he was brought in this morning. The doctor isn't sure when he will, either." Ryan's stomach turned and twisted.

"What about the kid?" Willy asked.

"Bobby's been really quiet all morning. He's the one who found Ed…" At this news, Ryan's stomach hurt even more. He had some memories–ones he'd tried to bury deep–that helped him relate to what Bobby was going through. "Bobby's aunt won't be able to fly out until tomorrow, either," Chyann continued. "She won't get here until Monday, so I offered to watch him over the weekend."

"Poor kid," Ryan said.

There was a long silence between the three of them before Chyann spoke again. "I need help, you guys," she whispered, tears glistening in her eyes. "I just…"

Willy put an arm around her. "We get it."

"We're right here," Ryan added, and Chyann nodded and rested her head against Willy's.

"Whatever you need, kid, you just let us know,"

Willy said in a low-effort mobster accent. Chyann laughed and jabbed him in the side. "Speakin' of kids," Willy continued, nodding at the window, "what's with the doll?"

Chyann shrugged. "It's a famous dummy some guy used to perform with a long time ago. Ed brought it home the other night." She took a drink of her espresso, and Ryan faced the window to give the doll another look. He couldn't explain why, but something about it seemed off.

"Anyway, Bobby and I have been here all morning," Chyann said with new composure. "I need to get him home and fed. If he'll eat, anyway."

"Food sounds good to me," Willy said.

"Great. I'll get Bobby, then." Chyann turned from them and stepped into the room. Ryan watched her as she walked over and knelt next to Bobby, but found he couldn't keep his stare from wandering over to the dummy.

"Is something wrong?" Boss asked.

"I'm not sure yet."

RYAN ATE HIS sandwich as he leaned against the doorway of the Flecks' living room, glancing over at the kitchen. Chyann had mentioned over the phone earlier that the room had flooded, and it definitely looked like it. Although the water was gone, the floor seemed to be peeling in some places, primarily beneath the sink.

Chyann was kneeling next to Bobby, who sat at the kitchen table. The dummy–Woody was his name, apparently–sat next to Bobby. Chyann had been speaking to the boy, but he hadn't said anything. He wouldn't even look at her. He just ate his sandwich without answering any of her questions.

In fact, Bobby had been quiet since they'd left the hospital. They had taken the bus home, and even then Bobby had refused to speak. It didn't surprise Ryan, though. The ten-year-old had gone through something awful. He had probably shut down, terrified for his father.

After many attempts to talk to the boy, Chyann stood and walked toward Ryan. She stopped next to him in the doorway. "I wish he'd talk to me," she said.

"Well," Willy started from behind them, "his dad *is* in the hospital. Maybe leave him alone for a bit and he'll come around." Ryan looked back to see Willy resting on the couch, his dirty plate set aside on the coffee table. He'd already eaten three sandwiches and had wanted a fourth, but Chyann had told him no. Otherwise, they would have run out of bread.

"No, it's not like Bobby to act this way," Chyann argued. "I mean, like, he's avoiding eye contact altogether. He's ignoring me on purpose." Ryan raised a brow. Considering how close Chyann and Bobby seemed to be, it didn't sound like Bobby to outright ignore her even when he was upset.

"Ohhh," Willy whispered.

Ryan took the last bite of his sandwich. Once he

finished it, he brushed off his hands and motioned to Bobby. "Mind if I try?"

"Go ahead," Chyann said.

With that, Ryan entered the kitchen and took a seat directly across from the ten-year-old at the table. "Hey, Bobby." The boy continued eating, his blank eyes trained on something past Ryan's head. "Sorry to hear about your dad," Ryan continued. "I can't imagine what you're going through." Bobby took another bite, unresponsive. It was almost as if he was in some sort of trance, locked in a repeating pattern of movement.

Ryan shifted his attention to Woody. The first time he'd seen the doll, he hadn't noticed the purple eyes. They gleamed under the light, seemingly innocent enough. But the more Ryan looked into them, the more uneasy he became.

In an effort to get Bobby to talk, Ryan reached for Woody. "Who's your friend here?" He grabbed the dummy by the arm.

"*NO!*" Bobby screamed, dropping his sandwich. The boy snatched Woody from Ryan and released a volley of shrieks that made Ryan jump in his seat. Bobby pulled the dummy close, staring hard at Ryan for the first time today. Desperation and fear laced the boy's expression. "You can't touch him." He set Woody back down on the chair.

"Sorry," Ryan responded. Bobby adjusted Woody's tie and jacket, then picked up his sandwich and resumed staring into space.

Ryan wasn't sure what to say. He glanced over his shoulder at Chyann and Willy standing in the doorway. They watched Ryan and Bobby, eyes wide.

Ryan turned back to Bobby and patted the table. "Good talk." He climbed to his feet and hurried to the living room, gesturing for Chyann and Willy to go in there, too. Ryan looked back at Bobby to see the boy lower his ear to Woody's lips, then nod as if in agreement to something the dummy said.

"*Very strange,*" Boss said in Ryan's mind. Ryan agreed, but he'd talk to Boss later; right now he needed to ask Chyann some questions.

"What did you say was up with that doll again?" he whispered as the three of them stopped near the couch.

"Some guy used to perform with it at the old town theater," she whispered back.

"Is there a computer around here that we can use?"

"Upstairs in Ed's study. Why?"

"'Cause I wanna know more about your little houseguest over there." Ryan headed for the staircase, and Chyann and Willy followed him. Pretty soon all three of them were in Ed's study. Ryan and Willy huddled around Chyann as she logged onto the computer. Normally it was locked via password, but apparently Ed had given his code to her in case Bobby wanted to play games or something.

After a few minutes of searching the internet, Chyann clicked on a scanned photo of a thirty-year-old town newspaper. *JOHNNY JAMISON VANISHES BEFORE FINAL PERFORMANCE!* the headline said. The image under it featured a tall, skinny man that reminded Ryan of a skeleton with skin stretched over its bones. Woody the dummy sat in the skeletal man's lap.

"Johnny Jamison and Woody were once the main attraction at Wellington Theater," Chyann read aloud. "But after a year and a half of success, Johnny failed to appear for his latest performance and has cut all contact with management."

"So this dude," Willy chimed in, "was a Twilight Peak rock star. And he just... stopped?"

Chyann nodded. "Sounds like it."

"Why?"

"It doesn't say." She continued examining the article.

"Could there be another article that explains what happened?" Ryan asked, and Chyann clicked through a couple more issues before another headline caught their attention: *JAMISON PRIME SUSPECT IN DIS- APPEARANCE OF THREE CHILDREN.*

Chyann didn't read this one out loud. She didn't need to, really; the headline said it all. Ryan leaned in to inspect the words, and then decided to read them aloud himself. "Authorities say Asha, Tyson, and Richie Jamison have all been officially reported missing after failure to arrive at school the week fol- lowing Johnny Jamison's sudden leave from Welling- ton Theater. Jamison did not report any of his chil- dren missing despite being their primary caregiver.

Investigators have no leads regarding the where-abouts of the children at this time, and news will be shared as it becomes available."

Ryan uttered the last bit of the sentence quite slowly, a heavy feeling weighing down the room. He noticed Chyann's hands were shaking, just as they had been on the night they'd gone to the cemetery to dig up Adella Williams. Also, Sadie had told Ryan what happened following Chyann's incident with Todd during lunch recently. How Chyann had bro-ken down in the bathroom. How Chyann wasn't as "okay" as she seemed.

"So, what about the little dummy-guy?" Willy asked. "Is he haunted by dead kids or somethin'?"

"Dunno," Ryan answered. Truth be told, he had no idea what was going on with Woody. All he knew was that something about the doll wasn't right.

"Where did Johnny get it?" Willy asked.

"I don't think that's mentioned in any of these articles," Ryan said, scanning the screen for more details.

"Well, maybe we can go ask him in person," Willy suggested. "He still around?"

Chyann slammed her palms on the desk. "Guys, stop it!"

Willy seemed taken aback by her outburst. "Stop what?"

"Whatever it is you're doing!" she yelled. "This isn't another stupid ghost hunt, all right?"

"Chy, we're just trying to figure out what's wrong with that dummy," Ryan explained. "We didn't mean to upset you." She stood up and walked to the other side of the room, massaging her temples and taking short, shaky breaths. "You can't tell me there isn't something weird going on here," Ryan added.

Chyann spun on her heel and balled her fists at her sides. "There is *nothing* weird going on here. The stuff about the missing kids is a coincidence, and it's tragic and dark. Most history is, by the way, and that's all *this* is. Messed up history from our messed up town."

"Do you really believe that?" Ryan grilled. "After everything we've found out recently, do you really think this is nothing? Bobby, back in the kitchen. The way he was acting. Do you think that's nothing?"

"His dad is in the hospital," she countered.

"And what put him in there?"

"He… he slipped. His kitchen was flooded. I already told you."

"And the muscle damage?" A long pause from Chyann. She crossed her arms, her hands still trembling. "People don't just get randomly electrocuted," Ryan went on. "You never told us how that happened."

Chyann glowered at Ryan, and he could tell she was trying to form an answer to his question. He could also tell she was afraid. "Say I find the address," she started. "Say Johnny is still around. What then?" There was an icy tone in her voice, a tone Ryan had only heard on rare occasions–when he and Willy had wanted to go cliff jumping and she'd been strongly against the idea, for instance. When Willy had gotten the three of them kicked out of her favorite store because he'd been caught stealing a candy bar. When the search for her missing sister had concluded.

This tone meant Chyann wasn't in the mood for jokes. She wasn't in the mood for debates, either. Even so, Ryan couldn't back down. He had to do something about Woody–he and his friends were probably the only ones who suspected anything was wrong with the dummy–and he needed Chyann's help.

"If Johnny is still around, then we'll talk to him," Ryan stated. "We'll find out where Woody came from and what's wrong with him."

"*You'll* talk to Johnny," Chyann corrected. "*I* don't want any part of this."

"Come on, Chy," Willy said.

"No!" Chyann yelled again, her cheeks flushing with anger. "I don't care about any of this. I'll find out where the guy lives or lived or whether he's in prison, but after that, you're on your own. I am not some monster hunter like Ryan's grandpa. I'm a seventeen-year-old girl, and this crazy shit is not going to be part of my life. Got it?"

Ryan thought back to the other times he'd seen Chyann angry–in the past, she'd always teared up. However, there were no tears in her eyes right now. He recalled Sadie's description regarding what she and Chyann had discussed in the bathroom as well. *Chy really isn't herself lately…*

There was a long, silent pause. Honestly, Ryan would have said something, but he was too caught up in the realization that Chyann was really, truly, horribly distressed, and he couldn't formulate a response. Willy wasn't much help, either.

A familiar flash blinded Ryan momentarily, a ghostly visage forming over the left half of his face. It was Boss. The Ooawan looked at Chyann. "Take a deep breath, child. You're clearly upset and unprepared to tackle another monster so soon." Boss's words seemed to calm Chyann. Her shoulders relaxed, her gaze falling to the floor. "Do what you can to find out where this Jamison character is located," Boss continued, "and the rest of us will take things from there. You can stay behind, if you wish." Chyann nodded. Even though her head was lowered, Ryan could tell she had begun to cry.

"Yeah, all right," Willy piped up. "We know you've been dealin' with some stuff lately, Chy. If you need to sit this one out, then we've got it."

Ryan swallowed hard, guilty for pushing Chyann so hard. Willy and Boss were right. Right now she didn't have it in her to deal with this, and no one should force her to try. "Ditto," he said. "Take all the time you need to get things sorted. I'm sorry."

She offered him a nod, and he caught sight of the streaks running down her cheeks. Heart aching for his hurting friend, Ryan stepped toward her and enveloped her in a hug. Willy followed suit. She squeezed them tight before pulling away. "Just please see if you can find anything on Jamison," Ryan said. "We can keep an eye on Bobby until you're done."

Chyann avoided eye contact, shuffling over to the computer and taking a seat. Ryan turned to Willy, and they exchanged looks of concern. They didn't have to say a word to know what the other was thinking: *I'm worried about her.*

For now, all they could do was try to make things easier until she was ready to face the truth–that monsters were real, that someone needed to fight them.

However, considering her outburst on the matter, Ryan wondered if she'd ever be ready to face it.

IT TOOK ABOUT half an hour for Chyann to come downstairs from the study. Bobby was sitting on the living room floor, watching a movie about a lost dog, and Woody was perched next to him. All the while, Ryan and Willy supervised from the couch, but Bobby acted as if they weren't there.

Ryan guessed the movie Bobby was watching was pretty old. He hadn't heard of it, but he imagined he had been a kid himself during its release. Just as the animal control officer pursuing the main character and his smaller dog sidekick fell into a river and began drifting down dangerous rapids, Chyann stormed into the living room. She stomped over to Bobby, snatched Woody from him, and headed for the hall.

"Chyann, *no!*" Bobby screeched, leaping to his feet and chasing after her.

Chyann spun around and pointed a stern finger at Bobby. "That's enough. Go get your shoes and coat."

"But I–"

"Shoes. And. Coat."

Ryan's eyes went wide with surprise. What had gotten into her all of a sudden? He glanced at Bobby, terror coming over the boy's expression. But whether it was from the tone in Chyann's voice or something else entirely, Ryan couldn't be sure.

Chyann stomped up the stairs, Woody in tow. "What's going on?" Willy asked.

"I'm not sure," Ryan replied. They stood and ran after her.

When they reached the top of the steps and started down the hall, Ryan saw Chyann in what he presumed was Ed's bedroom. She stuffed Woody into an old wooden trunk, slammed the lid shut, and latched the top. *That must be the case Woody came with*, Ryan realized, and Chyann dragged it toward them.

"What's the deal?" Willy blurted as Chyann passed him.

She stopped to catch her breath. "I found an address. We all go. If we find Jamison, he's taking this stupid firewood back, and we'll be done with it." Ryan couldn't believe this change in Chyann. Earlier, she hadn't been able to keep her composure, but now she possessed an aura of unbreakable determination.

Willy shrugged casually. "Sounds like a hot plan to me."

A whine came from somewhere in the room, and Ryan's heart almost stopped as something rose from beneath the bed. However, his panic quickly dissipated when he realized it was just a dog.

"That's Davey," Chyann said as the German shepherd stared at them. Davey's ears were pressed against his head, his tail low. He cried out a second time and returned to his spot under the bed. "Let's get Bobby and go," Chyann continued, walking down the hall toward Bobby's room.

Ryan glanced at the bed. *Dogs are usually pretty sensitive to the supernatural*, he thought. *Yet another thing that confirms something is wrong here.* He exited the room and followed his friends as Davey whined once more.

In the middle of the hall, Chyann zipped up Bobby's jacket and took his hand. "Come on," she ordered. "Will, can you get the trunk?"

"Yes, sir," Willy replied with a salute. Chyann and Bobby hurried past Willy, and Ryan hastened after them.

"Hey, you know you don't have to do this, right?" Ryan said.

"Yeah, I do," she snapped. "'Cause if something goes wrong and you guys get hurt, I don't think I'd ever get over that." They arrived at the front door and stopped to wait for Willy. "Besides, sitting here feeling sorry for myself isn't gonna solve anything either, so..." She looked around for a few moments before locking eyes with Ryan, though she still held her head low and didn't maintain eye contact for long.

Willy stumbled down the last few steps, hauling Woody's trunk behind himself. "Okay, boys and girls, let's go house hunting."

CHAPTER SEVEN

THE STREET RYAN FOLLOWED Chyann down was old. He hadn't been to this side of town often. Many of the houses were abandoned, deemed unsafe to reside in. The pavement was cracked, riddled with potholes so deep your car could get stuck in them. Many streetlights were burnt out, some missing bulbs completely.

When Ryan wasn't tripping on the weeds that tangled over the sidewalks, he watched Chyann. *I'm wondering if I should have asked her to stay behind*, he thought.

"My village had a saying," Boss chimed in from the back of Ryan's mind. *"The elders taught it to us at an early age. 'On leforvel wesk.'"* The words sounded

strange to Ryan, since Boss hadn't discussed much of the Ooawan culture and language with him. *"It means 'the strong will survive.'"*

"Like survival of the fittest?" Ryan asked.

"Aye. My people believed that if you were too slow to keep up with everyone else, you wouldn't survive long. Falling behind meant death was bound to happen."

"You believed that?"

"It might sound silly, but it was our culture. Many Ooawans fell over the years as other villagers surpassed them. Disease, accidents, killings during a hunt–all contributed to the village's death count. We took care of one another as best we could, of course, but some things were out of our control."

"Why bring this up?" Ryan asked, eager for Boss to get to the point.

"Because of Chyann," Boss explained. *"Perhaps she doesn't want to be left behind."*

The Ooawan's suggestion made sense to Ryan. Whenever he and Willy had discovered a new hobby, Chyann had always tried to learn it with them–sports, culinary arts, video games, you name it. Years ago, he and Willy had even attempted to learn parkour, and when Chyann had joined in, she'd surpassed both of them.

"This is it," Chyann suddenly announced, her voice cutting through Ryan's thoughts and bringing him back to reality. They were standing before a small old house. Ryan guessed it was maybe a one-bedroom. A rust-coated fence surrounded the yard, the dead grass adorned with multiple *NO TRESPASSING* signs. The beige-colored paint–what little of it that remained, at least–was peeling, falling from the house's sides, the brown-tiled roof in desperate need of repair. One of the front windows had been cracked in the shape of a spiderweb, held together from the inside by a mess of thin duct tape.

"What a bachelor pad," Willy said with a hint of sarcasm.

"Does anyone even live here?" Ryan asked.

Chyann shrugged. "This is the only address I could find, so let's hurry and get this over with." She approached the gate and tried to open it, but there was a large chain padlocked around it that allowed no room for it to slide open even a bit. However, the chain didn't seem to do much to deter visitors. Chyann lifted Bobby up, helped him climb over the fence, and then did so herself.

Ryan walked up to the chest-height fence and followed Chyann and Bobby over it with ease. Willy struggled to lift the trunk up and over, so Ryan took it from him instead. It really was heavier than it looked, almost as if it were filled with cinder blocks rather than a ventriloquist dummy. Once Willy reached the other side, Ryan decided to help him carry it the rest of the way.

They followed Chyann across the yard, up the porch, and toward the entryway. Chyann opened the ripped screen door and knocked hard on the wooden one behind it.

The knocks echoed down the empty street. Ryan hadn't realized it until now, but the whole neighborhood was deathly quiet. There weren't any vehicles–or people, for that matter–in sight.

No one answered the door. Chyann pounded on it again, the sound bouncing off nearby houses. It was as though they'd entered a ghost town.

Finally, Ryan heard locks and chains working on the other side of the door. It swung open. The pale, skeletal face of a man peeked out from the darkness inside. "Go away," he croaked. He sounded as if he'd been gargling gravel.

"Johnny Jamison?" Chyann asked. Despite the man's appearance and voice, her confidence hadn't wavered. Considering how much her mood had flip-flopped today, Ryan wasn't sure if that was worrisome or impressive.

"Johnny Jamison," the man repeated. "What do you want with him?"

"I'm Chyann. This is Bobby, and these two are Ryan and Willy."

"Nice to meet you," the man said in a mocking tone. "Now get off my porch." He tried to slam the door shut, but Chyann stuck her shoe between the door and the frame.

"Bobby's dad found Johnny's old dummy," Chyann went on, "and now he's in the hospital. We need help." The icy tone had crept back into her voice, but after a short pause, she dropped it. "Please?"

The man didn't reply for a long time. Ryan tried to see inside, to get a better look at the guy, but he was hiding behind the door. Without warning, he kicked

Chyann's foot out of the way and slammed the door shut before she could stop it again.

Ryan pressed his lips into a thin line. This was their only lead, their only shot at some answers regarding what was going on.

Chyann lowered her head, then raised it again. Ryan figured she'd have been relieved. After all, this was all they had to go on, and it hadn't panned out. Instead, she seemed more disappointed than he was.

Willy's nostrils flared. "Great. Now what?"

As if in response to Willy's question, Ryan heard more locks and chains working behind the front door of the house. It swung open again, all the way this time, revealing the man inside. He was tall and inhumanly thin, scraps of brown hair clinging to his scalp. Dark bags hung beneath his deep-set eyes, as if he hadn't slept properly in years. He wore a white tank top and baggy jeans.

The man stared down at them, motioning for them to enter. "Hurry up before I change my mind." Chyann grabbed Bobby's hand and led the boy inside. Ryan helped Willy carry the trunk into the house, and the man closed the door behind them.

Ryan and Willy followed Chyann into a big, open living room that housed a recliner, an electric fan, and a TV playing a black-and-white movie. The room had to have taken up ninety percent of the house's total living space, and Ryan was surprised to see that despite the home's shabby exterior, the interior was immaculate. Everything was clean and organized.

Ryan and Willy rested the trunk in the center of the room, and Ryan continued to examine their surroundings. The carpet was light-brown, almost the color of oatmeal. Photos of who Ryan assumed were this man's family members lined the shelves, and the entertainment center housing the TV also held a VHS player and a bunch of classic movies. On the far right side of the room there was another doorway, and, next to that, another shelf. This shelf was mounted high on the wall, and three infant-sized dolls sat on it–two boys, one girl, their features and clothing pristine.

The man plopped down in his recliner. "So, you found my dummy, huh?" Ryan squinted at the man. They couldn't have seen it before, but now, in the proper light, it was easier to discern. Yes, this man was thinner, older, and lacking the head of hair he'd had thirty years prior. But he was, without a doubt, Johnny Jamison.

"That's right," Chyann said, sliding the trunk toward Johnny. "And I want you to take this ugly thing back." She began to unlatch the lid, and Johnny didn't seem fazed in the slightest. She popped the lid open, then yelped and scrambled backward, a German shepherd leaping out from the trunk.

"Davey!" Bobby exclaimed as the dog hurried toward him.

"Oh, you found him, all right," Johnny said with a chuckle. Chyann stared at the dog in surprise and hastened over to the trunk to look inside. Ryan glanced into it as well, finding it empty. Woody was gone.

Chyann's cheeks paled. "But, he…"

"Relax, kid," Johnny said, raising a hand. "I recognize the case." He leaned toward Bobby, looking over the boy while Davey mercilessly licked his face. "Dad's not doing so well, huh?" Bobby shook his head sadly. "And what did Woody tell you?"

It took Bobby a while to answer. Once the dog had stopped assaulting his cheek with slobber, he spoke. "Woody told me not to tell Chyann what was going on. To do what he said, or he would hurt me like he hurt my dad." Tears streamed down the boy's face.

Johnny nodded, his expression that of understanding. "He told my little girl something like that, once upon a time."

"That's enough," Chyann said, stepping between Johnny and Bobby. "We need answers."

"Of course you do." Johnny laughed, leaning back in his chair. "What the hell else would you be here for?"

"What's the deal with this stupid doll?" she asked, but it sounded more like a demand.

Johnny threw his hands in the air. "Don't you get it yet? He isn't just some 'stupid doll,' kid. Woody is something else. Something… evil. He's been around for a very long time."

"Is he haunted?" Willy inquired.

"Not even close." Johnny stared off into space. "He's a living, walking, talking little nightmare. He could have been a whole lot worse, though, no thanks to me."

Ryan cocked his head. "What do you mean?"

"Back in the day, when I was performing at Wellington, I thought Woody was just a regular dummy. When he first spoke to me, I was, uhh…" He cleared his throat with a disgustingly wet cough before continuing. "Let's just say I was surprised. He told me he wasn't really a dummy, that he'd been trapped in a dummy's body some odd years ago by a curse. He said the only way to free him was to get his heart from the sorcerer who'd imprisoned him. He'd let me continue using him for performances so long as I helped him get free. That was the deal."

There was disappointment in Johnny's voice now. He chuckled dryly a couple of times before looking at Chyann. "How stupid I was. While I was breaking my back trying to find his stupid heart, he was ordering my children around, manipulating them when I wasn't there. He turned them into his slaves." Johnny paused to pour himself a drink on the tiny table next to him. Alcohol trickled into the glass and down his throat in such a quick sequence that Ryan wondered whether he'd thought about doing it or if it was pure muscle memory.

"I called a friend to help me find that damn heart," Johnny continued. "Even had a secret chamber installed in my dressing room to hold all my information on it. But the closer I got to it, the more aggressive Woody became with me. When we finally found the heart…" He trailed off, glanced down at what was left in his glass, and started to pour more. As Johnny continued, Ryan noticed Willy wandering around the room, examining the shelves and furniture. "Let's just say all hell broke loose. My friend–the one who helped me find the heart–he was kind enough to inform me that Woody was up to no good. And when I refused to give the little shit his heart, he lost his mind. Pulled a knife on me. Stole the thing. Said he was gonna move himself out of the dummy body and into– Hey!"

Fury overcame Johnny's face, and Ryan spun around to find Willy holding one of the dolls from the shelf nearby. "Don't touch that!" Johnny yelled, jumping up from his chair. He crossed the room so quickly it was as though he'd teleported from one side to the other. He snatched the doll from Willy's hands and cradled it to his chest.

Willy put up his hands in defense. "Sorry. My bad."

Johnny gently brushed some hair from the doll's face and placed it back on the shelf. After a few minutes he resumed talking, but he was quiet now, his tone somber. "I called my friend. He stopped Woody. Got the heart away from him. But... by then it was too late. He took my children away from me."

Realization flooded through Ryan, his breath catching in his throat. He stared hard at the dolls, then at Johnny, then again at the dolls. *The kids were never found. That couldn't mean...* "Wait a minute," he said. "You mean those dolls..."

"They're my children," Johnny confirmed. "Woody turned my children into dolls." Willy's eyes went big. He took a step back, wiping his hands on his pants.

"*What?*" Chyann cried, her face filled with horror.

Johnny turned to her, meeting her terrified expression with one of acceptance. "I guess Woody figured if I wouldn't let him have his heart, then he wouldn't let me have my kids. After he took my children from me, I hauled him to Wellington in that very case. I locked him in my secret room. I hoped he would stay there at least until after I was dead, but–"

"Why didn't you just destroy him?" Chyann interjected.

Johnny scowled. "Don't you think I tried? Fire, saws, dynamite. You name it, I tried it. You can't destroy that monstrosity." An exhausted sigh escaped his lips, and he ran a hand over the side of his face. "Lord knows Magnus and I tried…"

"What?" Ryan exclaimed. "Did you say Magnus?"

Johnny gave Ryan a confused look. "Yeah? So?"

"Magnus was my grandfather," Ryan replied. "We kind of just found out he used to do this sort of thing. Hunt monsters, I mean."

Johnny cracked a smile and shook his head. "Well I'll be shot dead. Probably shouldn't let that detail slip in front of Woody. He holds a grudge like nobody's business. If he's gotten free, then I guess it's only a matter of time before he pays me a visit, too."

Chyann put her hands on her hips. "There's gotta be a way to stop him."

"You don't stop him," Johnny said. "You *trap* him."

"What about his heart?" she blurted. She seemed to want to say more, but Johnny wouldn't let her.

"*You keep that thing as far away from Woody as possible!*" he screamed, pointing a slender finger at Chyann. "Nothing good will come if he gets ahold of it. Without the heart, he's just a walking dummy. But with the heart, he has power." Johnny pointed at the dolls on the shelf. "That is just a taste of what Woody's capable of when he's whole again."

"We'll stop him," Chyann vowed. "Maybe you couldn't find a way to destroy him, but *we* will." There was confidence in her words, and they invigorated Ryan. It brought him back to the moment in the lot behind the school, when he had refused to give up Boss to Steve Helsing. *Chy's right*, he thought. *They couldn't find a way to stop Woody, but we can do it.*

However, what Johnny did next shattered all of their conviction.

Johnny laughed. It was a deep, guttural sound that echoed off the walls of the living room. That drowned out the sound of the TV. It smashed through Chyann's bravado, her shoulders slumping low. Johnny laughed like this for several minutes straight.

When Johnny finally did stop, he made eye contact with Chyann and smiled. Not with smugness, not with happiness. It was a grin of confidence, one that matched the tone of his voice as he uttered his next words. "Good luck with that, kid."

CHAPTER EIGHT

CHYANN GRASPED BOBBY'S HAND tight as she led him down the street toward his house. Ryan and Willy walked ahead of them. Meanwhile, Davey trotted beside them. Willy adjusted the trunk, which he carried on his back as he walked. Chyann figured it was a lot less heavy now that it didn't have a full-grown German shepherd inside of it.

After Johnny Jamison had laughed in their faces, he'd kicked them out of his house and sent them on their way. And, honestly, that had been completely fine with Chyann. It wasn't like they were going to get any more information out of him, anyway. He'd told them plenty. If they could handle the vengeful spirit of Adella Williams, they could handle an evil dummy.

There had to be a way to destroy Woody; Chyann was sure of it. She just needed to do what… well, what Magnus hadn't been able to do.

The more she thought about the situation, the less she believed in herself. She'd decided earlier today that she wasn't going to make the boys do this alone, even if she'd rather stay out of it. And that meant she was part of this now. She needed to see it through to the end, but how was she going to be able to? Keeping herself together had been hard enough after Adella. How would surviving Woody affect her later on?

"I'm scared," Bobby whispered to her.

She pulled him closer, wrapping an arm around him as they walked. "Me too."

"Hey," Willy started, "don't let Johnny freak you guys out. His jigsaw puzzle is a few pieces short, if you know what I mean."

"It doesn't matter whether Johnny is crazy or not," Ryan said. "We need to make sure we find that heart before Woody does."

"How is Johnny *not* crazy, man?" Willy argued. "Woody's a *doll*. What's gonna stop me from drop-kickin' his little ass across a room?"

"If we're lucky," Ryan replied, "nothing."

By this time, Chyann could see the Fleck home up ahead at the end of the street. The group walked in silence the rest of the way. Soon they reached the porch, and Chyann retrieved the spare key from underneath the rug in front of the door. The key was always located within a small hole that had been carved into one of the boards. She unlocked the door, put the key back, and stepped inside.

The sun was setting behind them, its rays casting a soft pink light into the house. The rooms looked dark, but from what Chyann could see, everything seemed to be in its rightful place.

Davey barked, pushing his way between everyone's legs and sprinting into the house. "Davey, come back!" Bobby called, but the dog had already vanished.

Chyann closed the door. Willy dropped the trunk in the entryway. Bobby squeezed Chyann's hand, and Ryan said, "Split up. Let's find him." With that, Ryan walked down the hall toward the stairs, while Willy headed left into the living room. Still clutching Bobby's hand, Chyann crept toward the kitchen.

As she stepped onto the linoleum, her shoes *squeak*ed. She flicked on the light switch, but the kitchen stayed dark. *A fuse must have blown downstairs*, she thought, then pulled her cell phone from her pocket and switched on the flashlight. The phone didn't illuminate the entire room, but she still appreciated the small glow it provided.

She started her search, throwing open cupboards and shining her cell under the table. "I'm sorry I wouldn't talk to you earlier," Bobby said. "Woody said he would hurt you, too…"

"It's okay, honey," Chyann reassured him, offering a smile. "He's not going to hurt anybody else, all right?" Bobby nodded twice, and Chyann resumed looking for Woody, her confidence slowly returning. *I can do this*, she thought, searching the counter now. *I can–*

She stopped. What she was looking at now sent shivers down her spine, chilled her to the bone.

A knife was missing from the top block of the knife box on the counter. Chyann began backing away, scanning more hiding spots in the kitchen for Woody.

Something cold and hard landed on her back. What felt like a wooden hand slammed into her cheek and wrapped around her throat. Then something sharp pierced through the flesh of her right shoulder.

She cried out. Not only in pain, but in surprise. "Famous last words, girly," the sinister, high-pitched voice of a man whispered in her ear. Her vision faded between red and black, and suddenly all she knew was agony. What must have been the missing knife twisted in her shoulder. Gritting her teeth, she managed to reach up and yank the blade free.

She spun to face her attacker, but a wooden fist collided with her cheek. She fell to the floor in a daze. Her vision blurred. She blinked, trying to clear it.

Just as she thought she might be recovering, something grabbed her by the ponytail and yanked her head back. Something cold–something that felt a lot like the steel blade of a knife–pressed against her cheek. Bobby stood a few paces away, his face in his hands.

Chyann's attacker had a firm grip on her hair so she couldn't move her head. Despite this, she managed to glance up, catching sight of purple irises glowing fiercely against the darkness of the kitchen. "You disobeyed me, Bobby," Woody hissed. "I told you what would happen if you didn't do as I said. Now I'm gonna have to hurt her."

"*No!*" Bobby screamed.

"*Yes!*" Woody yelled back. Chyann watched as Woody raised the knife high. She was still too dazed to react. Too shocked at seeing the doll talk and move on his own.

A loud bark sounded from somewhere in the kitchen, and a set of canine jaws clamped down on Woody's knife-wielding arm. "Hey, what's the big idea?" Woody cried. "Go find a piece of furniture to chew on, you overgrown rug!" Davey growled, twisting and thrashing as he yanked Woody away.

Chyann felt the dummy release her hair, and suddenly Bobby was at her side. She sat up and clutched her bleeding shoulder. Ryan and Willy appeared in the kitchen doorway.

The butcher knife clattered to the floor, and Chyann turned toward Davey and Woody. The dummy couldn't even stay on his feet; the dog shook him violently every time he tried to gain his balance.

"Now's our chance!" Ryan shouted, rushing toward the dummy. Willy followed his lead. The boys tackled the doll, shoving him to the floor. Davey kept hold of him as well.

Chyann struggled to her feet. "Stay back, Bobby," she said sternly, then headed for the dogpile. One hand pressed against her bleeding shoulder, she kicked the blade far from the action and pinned down Woody's free palm to keep him from slapping at the others.

"Hey, I need that," Woody said, feigning sadness.

"Get his legs, Will," Ryan ordered. "Pin him down."

Woody's brows knit in anger. "Hey, you on the legs! Watch it!"

"I'm tryin," Willy responded to Ryan. "He won't stop squirmin."

Woody writhed beneath their hands. "Easy on the jacket! It's a limited edition!" This time the doll actually sounded concerned.

Chyann pressed her knee down onto Woody's hand, the one she'd been holding, and grabbed his flailing legs. "Tie them together," she said. Despite the dummy's kicking, they managed to tie Woody's stuffing-filled legs into a tight knot.

"You'll hear from my podiatrist about this," Woody growled, still trying to shake himself loose.

An idea struck Chyann suddenly, and she swung around to face Bobby. "Go get the trunk and bring it in here," she said. Bobby only stood there, staring blankly at the scene before him. "Now, Bobby!" Only then did the boy hurry out of the room.

Woody snorted. "Do you really think that stupid box is gonna hold me? Don't make me laugh."

"Do you ever stop talking?" Willy replied.

"Do *you* ever stop being *ugly*?" the dummy countered. Willy leaned back, pausing his attempts to subdue Woody for a moment. He glanced over at Chyann, and she saw legitimate hurt in his eyes, which confused her. *You've been called way worse by actual people*, she thought. *But a living doll calling you ugly? That's the line that gets you, huh?*

Suddenly the hurt in Willy's eyes was gone. Now he just looked angry. He ripped Woody's arm from Davey's mouth, flipped the dummy facedown, and double knotted his arms behind his back.

"Now what?" Ryan said.

Willy glowered down at Woody. "I say we hang him from a tree and beat him until we see candy." Woody could only thrash in protest beneath their weight. Anything he said sounded muffled because his mouth was pressed against the floor.

Chyann turned to the doorway. Bobby scurried in, dragging Woody's trunk with him. He dropped it next to the three of them and undid the latches.

"Good goin', kid," Willy said, lifting Woody up off the floor by the knots they'd tied him into.

"You little brat," Woody hissed at Bobby. "You better sleep with one eye open tonight. You hear me?"

Willy dumped the doll into the trunk. "Get stuffed, blockhead," he said, and slammed the lid shut. Chyann latched the left side while Willy did the right, Woody hollering from inside the wooden prison. "Well," Willy continued, "what next?"

Chyann leaned back against the counter and slid down onto the floor, her breaths shaky. They'd gotten Woody into the trunk, but she had no idea what to do with him now. Not to mention she could hardly think because her shoulder throbbed with pain. She pulled her hand from it to see that blood had stained her skin and jacket. Lessons from her mother and a few survival courses began funneling back to her, and she realized her clothes had buffered what would have otherwise been a severe wound. The injury still needed attention if she didn't want it to get worse, though.

Bobby handed her her cell phone, its flashlight still shining. "You dropped this."

"Thanks," she said, taking the device and aiming it at her injury to investigate further. She pulled her jacket and shirt below her shoulder, revealing a still-bleeding gash. It appeared to have been a rather thin cut initially, but now it was wider and oval-shaped, and Chyann guessed that was because of the way Woody had twisted the knife before she'd managed to yank the blade free.

"You good?" Ryan asked. She glanced up to find both Ryan and Willy staring down at her. Initially, they must not have noticed she was bleeding, probably because the scuffle had been in the dark.

"I think so," she answered, carefully putting her shirt and jacket back into place. "He got me pretty good when he jumped out. I'd probably be a goner if it weren't for Davey." A concerned whine sounded from the other side of the kitchen. She couldn't see where the dog was, but she knew he was still in here.

She looked down at her hand. Blood stained her palm and wrist, as well as the majority of her jacket sleeve. This was her favorite coat, too, and it was going to take some effort to fix the hole. Not to mention she'd have to wash the blood out. Things like blood were such a pain to remove…

The thought of washing the coat–of water, more specifically–gave her a new idea. She realized what they needed to do with Woody. "Guys, do you know where Donkey Bridge is?" she asked.

Ryan nodded. "It's like fifteen minutes from here. Why?"

She climbed to her feet. "Grab the trunk. That's where we're taking Woody next."

Willy gave her his signature troublemaker smile and grabbed one of the trunk handles. Ryan seized the other end, and Chyann hastened to the front door as they hauled the box behind her, Bobby following close.

In no time they were outside, heading straight for Donkey Bridge.

CHAPTER NINE

IT TOOK NEARLY TWENTY minutes to reach the bridge, and night had already taken hold of the sky.

Just like most structures in Twilight Peak, Donkey Bridge was fashioned from rounded stone and brick, four arches that reminded Chyann of films set in medieval times holding it high above the river below. Although she had an irrational fear of the structure's thirty-six-foot-long path crumbling beneath her feet, she knew it was well-maintained.

The throbbing in her shoulder seemed to worsen, a shock wave of pain arcing down her arm. If she was lucky, this would all be over soon and she'd be able to patch it up. At least she wasn't carrying the trunk, though; Ryan and Willy were doing that. When they'd made it halfway to the bridge, Woody had started kicking at his case ferociously, and Ryan had nearly tripped when the box had slammed into him after an especially nasty jerk. And, although Chyann could hear Woody's sadistic giggles coming from the trunk, she chose not to pay attention to them.

"Dude, carry your end," Willy said to Ryan.

"I am," Ryan snapped. "Carry yours!" As the boys argued back and forth, Chyann stepped onto the stonework of Donkey Bridge, familiar paranoia settling in her mind.

They neared the center of the bridge. Chyann stopped next to the railing and peered over the edge. Water flowed calmly below, heading west as it journeyed down the mountain. It looked serene now, but Chyann knew it was anything but gentle downstream. If they dropped Woody into the water, he'd either crash into jagged rocks or be thrown down a waterfall. Either way, he was about to be reduced to splinters, even if he found a way to escape his trunk. No matter what, so long as they got him into the stream, he'd be torn apart.

Chyann's confidence quickly disappeared, however. "Ow!" Willy shouted. Chyann swung around, but the situation was already out of control. Willy clutched his stomach with his free hand, barely managing to hold on to Woody's trunk with the other. The box rammed into his gut again. He cried out in pain, dropping the handle. The trunk tumbled to his feet.

As the box hit stone, one of the latches snapped open. The lid's hinges came loose, and Woody hopped out onto the bridge. He raised his arms with the confidence of a showman. "*Ta-da!*" he sang triumphantly. "I'm free, and all I had to do was kick around and jump a bit."

Willy recovered quickly. He seized the trunk lid, ripped it off the rest of the way, and swatted Woody with it. The dummy rammed into the bridge railing with a loud *clunk* and sank to the ground in a heap.

Before anyone could celebrate the defeat, a crackling noise sounded in the air. Willy screamed, doubling over in pain.

Woody rose to his feet. It was then that Chyann saw what he had in hand. It was yellow, with wires running from it. They were shooting straight at Willy. *The Taser*, she thought. *My Taser.*

Woody cackled. "That never gets old." He turned toward her, a sinister glow in his purple eyes. Her stomach dropped. "Get over here, Bobby," the dummy commanded.

Bobby squeezed his arms around Chyann's leg, and Ryan stepped in front of them, shielding them from Woody. "Bobby isn't going anywhere with you," Ryan said.

Woody tilted his head back and laughed. It was sharp, high-pitched. It made Chyann's blood run cold. "He doesn't have a choice," Woody finally replied, and pointed the Taser at Willy. "And neither do you." Willy screamed in pain once again. "If the boy doesn't come," Woody continued, "I'll keep pressing this button until Sweater here gets deep-fried. *Inside and out.*"

Chyann couldn't help but shiver at Woody's words. She knew the Taser wasn't strong enough to cause any lasting damage, but if Woody kept at it until the battery pack burned out…

Willy continued wailing, writhing about on the ground. "Ticktock, kiddo," Woody called. "One order of snot-nosed brat, extra crispy!"

Chyann felt the grip on her leg release. Bobby was running away from her. "Bobby, no!" she cried.

But it was too late. The boy sprinted past Ryan, hurrying toward Woody. "Stop it!" Bobby said. "I'll go with you. Just stop hurting him."

Woody stared at Bobby for a moment, sizing him up as if trying to decide whether the boy was sincere. Chyann tried to go after Bobby, but Ryan stopped her. The pain of her stab wound flared, halting any attempt at fighting her way past him.

What felt like whole minutes passed before Woody tossed the Taser to the ground. "Let's go. We've got errands to run. Places to be." Bobby lowered his head and picked Woody up as though the doll were his younger sibling. Then the boy turned around, allowing Woody to face Chyann and Ryan one last time. "You see," Woody started, "Bobby and I have an understanding. An unbreakable bond, if you will. We're two peas in a pod. You never stood a chance."

Bobby glanced at Chyann, his eyes glittering beneath the moonlight. He wore a terrified expression.

"It's been fun," Woody went on, "but I've gotta r–" Before he could finish his rhyme, Bobby lunged

116

sideways–and flung Woody over the bridge's stone railing.

Chyann gasped in surprise, slapping a blood-soaked hand over her mouth. Woody must have been shocked as well; he released a volley of yells and curses before he was cut short by a *splash*.

Ryan hurried over to Bobby and Willy, and after taking the time to process what she'd just witnessed, Chyann did the same. When she reached Bobby's side, she knelt and hugged him tight. "Don't you ever scare me like that again," she said.

Bobby hugged her back. "I won't. Woody's gone now, right?"

"Yeah," Chyann replied. She laughed as she released Bobby. "You beat him, you little hero." He offered her a weak, exhausted smile. He must be tired, and she couldn't blame him. It had been an incredibly long and hard day for both of them.

"This might hurt," Ryan said from behind, and Chyann and Bobby turned that way. Ryan had his fingers wrapped around the Taser darts on Willy's chest.

Willy groaned. "Would you quit wussin' out and just pull the damn thi–" Ryan yanked at the darts. They came free, a sharp yipe escaping Willy's throat. "Thanks," Willy said with a sigh.

Ryan raised a palm. "How many fingers am I holding up?"

Willy swatted Ryan's hand away. "Shut up." He struggled to his feet, swaying back and forth.

Who knew a hunk of wood could be so dangerous? Chyann wondered, and headed toward the opposite side of the bridge to search for any signs of Woody below. *Better safe than sorry.*

The water flowed as it usually did–undisturbed. She hadn't heard Woody resurface, either, but she also couldn't see very well in the dark. If the dummy had been in the trunk when he'd fallen from the bridge, she wouldn't have had to worry at all.

Despite her concerns, she felt... at ease. As if the weight she'd been carrying for the past week had been lifted ever so slightly. Her surroundings were practically pitch-black from the night, sure, but her perspective was brighter. *Things are going to be okay*, she thought.

Ryan helped Willy hobble to her side. Bobby walked over as well, and they all looked down at the river. "Think that's it for the little termite bait?" Willy asked.

Ryan shrugged. "Dunno."

"He's a goner if he makes it to the waterfall," Chyann said. "That's for sure."

Ryan and Willy started shuffling away, arm in arm. "Let's get outta here," Ryan said. His voice sounded as tired as Chyann felt. She wasn't about to argue against the idea of returning to the Fleck house and giving some much-needed attention to her shoulder.

She checked her injury again as she followed the others off the bridge. The bleeding had slowed, but it still hadn't stopped. At this rate, she wondered whether she was exhausted due to her rollercoaster of a day, or if her body was succumbing to blood loss. *At least it won't take as long to get back to the house as it took to get here.*

She glanced at Willy, at how awkward his movements were after Woody's attack. If it weren't for Ryan, Willy probably wouldn't be able to walk at all.

At least, Chyann thought, *I hope it won't take that long.*

WHAT WAS PAIN? It had been so long since he'd felt that dreaded sensation. He had been trapped in this wooden vessel for too long. Even as sharp rocks struck him, even as tree branches impaled his torso, even as things unseen tore his arm from his body, he felt nothing.

There was no feeling, only force. Force that pushed and pulled him in various directions. He experienced no agony, no hunger, no desire for sleep.

It was all just *existence.*

His head hit another stone, and he heard an eardrum shatter as the river pitched him farther down the current.

Despite his predicament, he still couldn't believe Bobby had betrayed him, had thrown him off the side of that bridge. If he didn't have such grand plans for Bobby, the child would have joined him down here in the water.

More rocks against his head. *Clunk. Clunk. Clunk.* Now half his vision was gone. One of his eyes must have shattered, or perhaps it had been thrown from the socket altogether. And (he hadn't noticed this before, but suddenly it was hard to ignore) his legs were gone as well.

He deliberated upon his missing limbs for a moment. *The branch that impaled me must have ripped me in half when I wasn't paying attention*, he thought. But he wasn't upset with himself for missing such a detail. After all, it was difficult to focus on keeping his parts together in situations like this.

Not that keeping himself together mattered, anyway. Because it didn't. Nothing did. Even when he suddenly found himself airborne, nothing mattered. His magic would piece him back together soon enough.

As he tumbled through the air, he caught sight of the sky. The moon was hidden behind clouds, but the stars were bright. It was nice to look at them before he crashed into the river again. *That must have been the waterfall*, he thought, though he had no way to check. All he could see was black now. *Have I lost the other eye?*

It was a long time before the water finally seemed to slow, to settle, and it pushed him ashore, onto a bank of mud. At least he guessed it was mud, due to its squishiness beneath his remaining fingers.

A few moments later his vision returned. He had been correct; one of his eyes had shattered in the socket, but now it was back. He patted his face and noticed his nose was missing. *That just won't do. It's one of my best features.*

A chuckle rose in his throat. Did those kids really think throwing him in a river would stop him? They had gone looking for ol' Johnny Boy, hadn't they? Johnny would have told them it was pointless to try and destroy him.

Maybe they hadn't listened. Or maybe Johnny hadn't bothered telling them. Either way, Woody just needed to wait until he was whole again. Not like that would be an issue, though. Those kids weren't going anywhere anytime soon. If he could wait in a locked box for thirty years, he could wait an hour or two in the muck.

He turned and saw his missing fingers rolling through mud and grass. They attached themselves to his broken hand, the cracks sealing and vanishing. *Good as new.* He curled them a few times and sat up as best he could to glance around. His arm was already worming itself toward him from up the bank.

A serpentine movement in the water caught his eye. With any luck, that was one of his legs. He leaned back as his arm reattached itself. Thankfully, he could prop himself up now.

As he sat up, his bottom jaw came cruising out of the brush and bumped into him. He picked it up and lifted it to his head. It snapped into place.

Light glinted in the grass, and his other eye rolled to his side, just as his jaw had. All he had to do was put it back in the socket, and then he could *really* see.

It truly was a shame. Being stuck in this vessel had its perks, but the problem was it weakened him severely. He needed his heart. He couldn't reach full power without it.

I suppose agonizing over being stuck in here doesn't matter much, he thought, and it didn't. He wouldn't be stuck much longer. First he would retrieve his heart. Then he would make this town bow to him. Maybe he would even string up that kid, the one that stinks of ol' Magpie. Hey, the meddling codger caused heaps of trouble for him in the past, and somebody had to foot the bill. If he couldn't get back at Magnus, he'd have to find a surrogate. Sins of the grandfather, and all that.

Those kids weren't going to stop his plans. Especially if they were only going to try and break him. There was no "breaking" him, and he *couldn't wait* to be whole again so he could find them and inform them of that fact. For now, though, he had to wait.

And waiting, of course, was absolutely no problem at all.

CHYANN FINISHED WRAPPING the bandages around her shoulder. After she'd taken the time to clean and assess it, she'd discovered the stab wound hadn't been as severe as she'd initially thought. Most of the damage had come from Woody twisting the blade, but the injury itself wasn't very deep. Sadly, she couldn't do much for the pain aside from taking some painkillers.

She stood up from the closed toilet lid and reached for her shirt. The one she'd been wearing earlier was stained with blood, and she'd packed an extra in her overnight bag. Her jacket was another matter, unfortunately.

As she turned the shirt to get it facing the right way, she caught a glimpse of herself in the full-body mirror next to the sink. Her skin was pale, unusually so. Probably from the blood loss. Her hair was wild; the ponytail she'd tied it into that morning had come loose, strands of brown sticking out in every direction. Her bra and even her jeans were stained with splatters of scarlet. The only articles of fabric on her body untouched by blood were her pink-and-yellow striped socks.

Her gaze fell to the necklace she always wore. It was a black heart, silver in the center. Miraculously, there was no blood on it–at least, not as far as she could see. A good thing, too, considering it was all she had left of her missing sister, Cassidy. Mom had packed away Cassidy's belongings after authorities had called off the search for her. Chyann always told herself that was just her mother's way of coping, but it didn't make it hurt less.

Her throat tightened, but she fought against it, trying to breathe. A soft choking noise escaped her lips. *No*, she thought. *Stop. You don't have the time to sit around and cry right now.* Shoving the thoughts of her big sister from her head, she slipped on her clean shirt, grabbed the plastic bag containing her dirty one, and left the bathroom.

As she walked, aches plagued her body. It was a struggle to do so much as flip off the light switch on her way out the bathroom. Still, she wanted to check on Bobby before she herself rested. It was one thing for her to go through a day like today, but something else entirely for someone Bobby's age.

She tiptoed down the hallway and peered into Bobby's room. The ten-year-old lay on his bed, still fully clothed and fast asleep. He hadn't even turned on his night-light. Honestly, the sight of him like this brought her some relief. Maybe it meant there was hope for her, too, as far as sleeping was concerned.

She set down the plastic bag holding her unclean garment, crept over to Bobby, and wrapped a blanket around him before turning on his night-light and exiting the room. Then she picked up the bag again and headed down the hall.

As she descended the stairs, she saw Ryan and Willy standing by the front door. They turned to her as she neared the bottom of the steps. "How's the kid?" Willy asked.

Chyann shrugged. "Asleep for the moment. Hopefully he'll wake up thinking Woody was just a nightmare."

"We should be so lucky," Ryan replied. "What about you?" He jerked his head in her direction as he asked the question.

She raised her left hand to her shoulder. "Sore. But I'll live." Ryan's and Willy's expressions morphed into ones of relief, and Chyann realized they had their things gathered. She knit her brow. "Are you guys leaving?"

"Just for a bit," Ryan replied, nodding. "Gonna look through my grandpa's stuff and see if we can find any leads on Woody's heart."

The thought of being alone terrified Chyann, but she wanted to stay strong. Woody was gone. "Good idea," she said. "If Magnus was involved with stopping Woody before, he might know where the heart is."

They must have noticed her anxiety flaring, because they shared a quick, knowing glance. "One of us can stay behind with you," Ryan began. "If you want."

She would have liked to say, *"Yes, please stay."* But for some reason, a feeling like anger began boiling from within, and she replied, "What, you think I can't handle being alone for an hour?" The boys opened their mouths to speak, but she cut them off. "You guys go, get what you need, and come back. I can keep an eye on things here just fine."

"Are you sure?" Ryan asked.

"Yes," she answered, though her voice was shaking. "I'm sure."

She could tell by the way the boys were staring at her that they didn't believe her for a second. "We'll be back in a flash," Willy said. "Just call if you need us, and we'll turn around and come back."

"Lock up after we leave," Ryan said. "Don't let anyone or anything inside unless it's us." She fought the urge to roll her eyes. Ryan didn't have to tell her any of this. That was already her plan, whether one of them stayed or not.

"No problem," she replied.

Ryan and Willy turned to leave. Willy opened the front door, and as they stepped outside, Chyann blurted, "Just, uhh…" The words came out sounding much more worried than she'd intended. The boys swung around to face her. Her grip on the stair railing tightened. "Hurry back?"

They offered her easygoing smiles before heading outside. "We'll be back before you can sing the alphabet," Willy said. He shut the door, and then they were gone.

And she was alone. Again.

She wasted no time tossing the bag holding her soiled shirt aside and going room to room to lock each and every window. When she finished ten minutes later, she settled onto the couch.

The doors and windows were locked, all the blinds drawn. Bobby was asleep, and Ryan and Willy were out. She thought maybe she should eat, but food didn't sound very appealing. Besides, she couldn't be bothered to get up from this spot. She was too comfy.

Maybe I'll read some more of my book, she thought, and pulled the novel from her bag on the floor next to her. Yawning, she flipped it open and started reading. This would pass the time quickly, and before she knew it, the boys would be back.

REALITY WAS WEIRD—*At least, as far as Bobby was concerned.*

A moment ago he'd been standing in the kitchen, playing with Davey while he ate lunch. Then the dog had run upstairs and crawled underneath Dad's bed, which wasn't exactly out of character. Davey often slept there when he was scared, and sometimes Bobby would join him during thunderstorms.

This time was different, though. The sun had been shining, and the thunder had come so suddenly. It shook the house as Bobby ascended the stairs and ran to Dad's bedroom. He caught a glimpse of Davey's tail wiggling beneath the bed. It disappeared, and then a strange question echoed in his mind, What was I eating for lunch?

It was so... weird. He'd been eating his meal. It had been his and... wait.

Who had made him food in the first place? Nobody else was home with him besides Davey. Where was Dad?

Apparently, there wasn't time to think about it. Bobby was already crawling under the bed to get to Davey.

No sign of Davey. Not anywhere. But that couldn't be right, because the bed was up against a wall, so it wasn't as if the dog had anywhere else to go. Yet after Bobby looked around, he realized there was no wall. Not where there should have been, anyway. All he could see was black. An endless void of space beyond where the wall should have been.

That had to be where Davey had gone, and Bobby needed to get him back.

On and on the boy crawled. He called out Davey's

name, but the dog didn't come back. A few barks sounded in the distance, but that was all.

Hours passed, and still no sign of Davey. Not even a clump of hair or a pile of dog poop. Maybe I should have brought my lunch, *Bobby thought.* That way I could have bribed Davey with food and he would've come back.

Something cold and wet splashed onto the back of Bobby's head. What was that? *he wondered, scratching at his hair.* Could it be rain? *A storm had been brewing outside, but Bobby was under a bed.*

More water splattered onto Bobby's head. Drip, drop. Drip, drop. Drip, drop. *He rolled onto his back and stared up, intending to find the source of the liquid, but soon found only pitch-black.* Drip, drop. *More landed in his eye.* Drip, drop. *Then his nose.*

It was in this moment that Bobby realized he was dreaming, and reality crashed into him like a tidal wave. However, as soon as he opened his eyes, he wished he hadn't awoken at all.

Woody the dummy loomed over him, staring down with those glowing purple eyes. The doll's hair was no longer slicked back. Instead, a soaked, mud-covered mess stuck out from his head in all directions. His usually clean white suit was stained a murky green, layers of dried sludge clinging to it. Water droplets rolled off of him, one by one. *Drip, drop. Drip, drop. Drip, drop.*

One landed on Bobby's cheek, but he was too scared to move, to scream. He wondered–he *hoped*–that he hadn't actually woken up, that this was a nightmare.

"That wasn't very nice of you, Bobby," Woody hissed, his wooden lips slightly parted. "Throwin' me in the river." Bobby's breath caught in his throat, his stomach churning. "Didn't ya know?" Woody continued, his nose grazing Bobby's. "*Wood floats.*"

Bobby screamed, and Woody didn't try to stop him. All the dummy did was cackle.

CHAPTER TEN

CHYANN JOLTED AWAKE, HER book dropping to the floor. She wasn't sure when she'd fallen asleep or how long she'd slept. She also wasn't sure whether the scream she'd just heard had been real or part of a dream.

She sat up, pain shooting through her shoulder. She knew she'd at least slept long enough for her meds to wear off.

Shuddering, she remembered where she was. "Bobby?" she called, climbing off the couch. Was he the one who'd screamed? Worst-case scenarios flashed through her mind, and she rushed out of the living room and hurried up the stairs. After she almost slipped turning down the hall, she paused to look at the floor. It was soaked, but why?

She stifled a gasp, realizing the scream she'd heard couldn't have been part of her imagination. There were tiny, muddy footprints on the hardwood, and they led straight to Bobby's room.

Her pulse drummed in her ears. "Bobby!" She sprinted to his room and shoved open the door. Once her eyes adjusted to the darkness, she saw his bed was empty. A gentle breeze whispered to her through the open window, curtains flowing in and out.

Chyann's heart nearly stopped. Her lungs burned as she shouted Bobby's name over and over, though she couldn't hear herself do so. Everything was on mute right now.

She had to find Bobby. She had to find Bobby *immediately*. He was her responsibility, and because of her, he was...

She stepped back and slipped on mud. As she fell, she struck her bad shoulder on a dresser. The resulting sensation was agonizingly intense; her injury had no issue reminding her it was there.

Suddenly someone grabbed her, their grip tight on her arms. Despite the pain rattling her body, she thrashed against the assailant. Their grip tightened, holding her arms down, and she realized her eyes were shut. She forced them open, quickly realizing no one was attacking her. There wasn't some creature or an evil dummy prowling around the house. It was Ryan.

Ryan's face was drawn in concern, his lips moving fast, but Chyann couldn't process what he was saying. Behind Ryan, Willy hurried over to the open window and peered outside.

Ryan gave Chyann a gentle shake, and finally she could hear his voice over the sound of her own pounding heart. "What happened?" he asked. "Are you okay?" She nodded a few times, and Willy made his way to her side.

"The kid's gone," Willy said.

"Chy, what happened?" Ryan cried, his voice laced with panic.

She couldn't find the words right away. "I... I... I..."

"Breathe," Ryan told her. "Breathe."

She did as he said, gulping down air as she tried to collect herself. "I–I fell asleep. Bobby screamed. I rushed up here, but he..." Her vision blurred, a lump forming in her throat. "He's gone. Bobby's gone."

Ryan hugged her tight. "Just for now. We'll get him back, I swear."

"What now, then?" Willy asked. Ryan gave Chyann a reassuring squeeze before letting her go. She wiped her eyes, trying to bring her vision back into focus.

Ryan stood, fists balled. "Where would Woody go?"

Chyann allowed her hands to fall to her sides, her mind buzzing with fear. *No*, she thought. *Push the bad thoughts out of your head. Focus on the question.*

Once she did that, the answer was clear. "Johnny Jamison," she said, her voice cracking. "Woody would go to Johnny Jamison. The heart is what that maniac's after, right?"

"Probably," Ryan replied. "But Johnny has no clue where the heart is."

"Did Magnus?"

The corner of Ryan's mouth turned up in a slight smile. "He did. There was an entry in the journal about this. It was vague regarding where the heart's hidden, but Johnny gave it to my grandpa. Grandpa Magnus tried to destroy it, but no dice." He offered her a hand, and she took it. Pain flared in her shoulder as he pulled her to her feet; she had to grit her teeth to avoid crying out. "Grandpa figured since he couldn't destroy it," Ryan continued, "he'd hide it, and he put it in the last place Woody would look."

"Wellington freakin' Theater," Willy finished for Ryan. "Right under the little prick's nose."

"The only problem," Ryan added, "is that Grandpa didn't say where exactly in the theater he hid the heart. Just something about the 'Northside Star.'"

"We have no clue what that means, but I bet you ol' Jamison does," Willy said. "And if Night of the Living Nutcracker is already on his way to Jamison's place, then we gotta hurry."

As if on cue, familiar light flashed over the left side of Ryan's face, and Boss appeared. "We will intercept the dummy. You can stay here, if you wish," the Ooawan said to Chyann.

He sounded concerned, but Chyann didn't believe it was genuine. "What? No," she responded. "I'm coming with."

Ryan and Willy shared knowing looks. "You sure?" Ryan inquired.

She couldn't believe he was asking her this. "Are you kidding me? I was just out there with you guys! After I got stabbed, no less."

"I know, but we–"

"Stop treating me like some scared kid that needs coddling!" Her cheeks grew hot as she yelled. Ryan blinked in surprise, as did Boss.

Willy threw his hands in the air. "I know the situation's bad, but can everyone just take a sec to relax? Jeez."

They all went quiet. Several moments passed before Ryan spoke again. "If you wanna come, then let's go."

No one had to add anything else. Together, they hurried out of the house without another word. Then they were sprinting down the street, and Chyann couldn't help but feel as though they had formed a sort of rhythm doing this. *It's like the universe is playing a cruel joke on me*, she thought.

She'd believed that Adella would be the last of her supernatural encounters. That the strange events were over, that she would grow old with faded memories of the ghost in the house at the end of the street. Now here she was, running through neighborhoods to save her babysittee from an evil living doll.

Tears sprang into the corners of her eyes, but she forced them back with all the effort she could spare. Bobby needed her. The boys needed her. She wasn't about to let any of them go through this alone.

JOHNNY SAT IN his chair, staring at the television. He couldn't really tell what was on, though. Once those kids had left earlier today, he'd kept working on his bottle of whiskey. Only stopped when he'd run out.

His face felt hot, like there was fire burning behind his eyes and in his throat. As much as he wanted more alcohol, ice-cold water sounded better. There was a bottle next to his chair–there should be some water in it–and as he reached over to pick it up, he... Oh, it was empty.

He tossed the container to the floor with a flick of his wrist. *I'm gonna have to get up and fish a new bottle outta the fridge*, he thought. After all, bottled water was the only way to go out here. The city "water," if you could even call it that, had an extremely strange taste–at least in his neck of the woods, it did. As far as he was concerned, the only thing it was good for was washing, and even then he preferred the filtered stuff if given a choice.

It took most of his effort to lift himself from the chair, even more to keep himself from toppling over. His legs felt like jelly. They moved how he wanted, sure, but the action occurred whole seconds after the thought.

He swayed back and forth as he made it into the kitchen. Once he got there, he placed a hand on the counter and used it to steady himself as he walked the five or so steps across the floor to the fridge. It felt like a massive trek due to how slowly he had to move, but he couldn't go any faster unless he wanted to spend the night on the kitchen floor. Still, if he fell, it wouldn't have been the first time.

The fridge was cool to the touch, and it emitted chilly air even while closed. Johnny stood there a moment, just to soak in the soothing cold, before opening the fridge for more. *Wait,* he thought suddenly, *why was it cold before I opened the fridge?*

He glanced around, his vision fuzzy, everything shifting in and out of focus. He blinked a couple of times, staring hard at the curtain above the sink. Finally, his eyesight cleared enough to offer some answers. The window was wide open, a gentle breeze blowing in from outside.

It was then that Johnny heard the voice. The voice that had haunted him for the past twenty-eight years. "Howdy, partner," the voice hissed.

Johnny closed his eyes. He let out a long breath. Partly to calm himself. Mostly because he was still incredibly drunk and had begun to feel nauseous.

He cursed under his breath. The moment he'd been dreading for a very long time was upon him. He looked back, still leaning on the fridge, and saw two small figures standing before him. One was Woody, of course, and the other was the young boy who had been at his house earlier today along with those three teenagers.

Johnny couldn't help but chuckle at the sight of his old dummy. Woody's suit was ruined and stained, his messy hair covered with mud. He glared at Johnny.

"Rough night?" Johnny asked with a chuckle, turning his body toward them. He almost fell doing so, and found he needed to continue leaning on the fridge to stay upright. "You look like shit."

"You're one to talk," Woody replied. "At least I'm still the handsome one. You just got uglier while I was gone."

Johnny burst into a fit of laughter at this comment, though he wasn't sure why. He lost his balance. Ended up on the floor.

Woody stepped forward. He was only inches away from Johnny now. "Johnny, Johnny, Johnny," he started, feigning concern, "what happened to ya?"

"You," Johnny managed to spit out between laughs. "You happened to me. Took my kids, my life. I can't even sleep without seeing your face." As he spoke, his chest ached. But funnily enough, he couldn't bring himself to cry. In fact, a part of him felt at peace. Maybe it was the alcohol. Shouldn't he be scared?

Woody beamed. "What can I say? I'm unforgetta-ble." He giggled at his own joke and elbowed the boy behind him. The boy, Johnny realized, was wearing his pajamas. *What, did that girl just throw Woody into a river and tuck the kid into bed ten minutes later?* Johnny thought. *Is she stupid? I told her... Nevermind. It doesn't matter now.* And it didn't. Johnny could read the room, and he knew what was coming.

Woody pulled a gleaming butcher knife from his suit jacket. "Now, let's get down to business. Shall we?"

CHYANN SPRINTED DOWN the cracked pavement, Johnny Jamison's house only a block away. She ran ahead of Ryan and Willy since she still remembered where it was located. The sounds of sneakers pounding against the sidewalk told her the boys were right behind her.

Unfortunately, the pain in her shoulder had yet to fade. She hadn't exactly had the time to stop and take a painkiller on her way out of the Flecks' place. As much as it hurt, she was going to have to tough it out for now.

"We're almost there," she said as the residence came into view. When they arrived, Chyann wasted no time climbing up and over the gate. However, a worrisome sight welcomed her back to the decrepit house. The front door was halfway open, light spilling out from inside.

Ryan and Willy clambered over the fence, but she

didn't wait for them. By the time they made it to the fence, she was already inside the house.

The television played another old black-and-white film, its volume low, and the lamp on the table next to Johnny's chair casted dim light across the room.

There was no sign of Johnny in here. The other doorways were dark, but Chyann needed to find him. "Mr. Jamison," she called out, and Ryan and Willy stumbled into the house. "Mr. Jamison!" she repeated, much louder this time, as she headed into the next room.

She felt around for the light switch. Once she located it, she turned it on. The bulbs overhead flickered to life.

When she saw the scene before her, she pressed a hand over her mouth, stifling the scream that threatened to escape her lips.

She was in the kitchen. It would have been a nice, clean white room, if it weren't for the fact that dark-red fluid had been splattered everywhere. Johnny was slumped against the fridge, cuts covering his face, torso, and arms, his eyes shut tight. His fingers had been severed from his hands, and they lay in pools of scarlet next to him. Worst of all, there was a vicious gash in his chest, blood seeping from the wound.

Chyann's stomach churned, sour bile rising in her throat. She clamped her eyes shut. *Maybe, if I just keep them closed, I can keep the image from being burned in my mind*, she thought, but deep down she knew it would haunt her forever.

"Holy shit," Willy whispered behind her. A hand gripped her shoulder, and she turned toward whoever it belonged to. She opened her eyes, found Ryan.

She turned back toward the kitchen. *It's real. Johnny Jamison is dead.* She stepped back and bumped into Ryan. He wrapped an arm around her and turned her away from the grisly scene.

What were they supposed to do now? They knew the heart was inside Wellington Theater, but Woody still had Bobby, and now Johnny was…

A strange noise sounded in the kitchen, and Chyann perked up. It seemed to catch Ryan's attention as well, because he did the same. The sound came a second time, and Chyann realized what it sounded like–a cough mixed with a choke. A disgustingly wet noise.

She spun around to find Johnny still alive, coughing up blood all over his chest.

Tentatively, she stepped toward him. "Mr. Jamison," she said. Once she reached his side, she knelt down next to him, glancing at his ruined chest. *I need to call an ambulance*, she thought. But from what she could see, even if she got help, Johnny wouldn't be of this world for much longer.

Johnny's eyes opened slightly. "Who's there?" he asked, crimson welling in his mouth.

"It's Chyann," she answered. "I was here earlier today."

Johnny closed his eyes again, and a wet chuckle escaped his lips. Fresh blood dribbled down his chin. "Right, right. The girl who insisted on destroying the..." He trailed off, fell into another fit of hacking before speaking again. "And how's that workin' out for ya?"

"It..." Chyann paused. "It's not going well."

"Thought not."

She bit her lip. "How do we stop him?"

"I told you already. You have to trap him."

"But how?"

Johnny wheezed, his body spasming. "I'm sure you kids will figure something out. You're already followin' in Magnus's footsteps. Just..." He coughed a few times more, and it sounded as if his throat were being torn apart by a garden rake. "Just try something a little more permanent than what Magnus and I managed to pull off, huh?"

"We will," Chyann whispered.

"Did you ever find the heart?" Johnny continued, the strength of his voice fading. "Woody knows it's in the theater. He had to start cuttin' off my fingers before I finally told him. Probably a good thing I have no idea where in the theater it actually is."

"The heart is... I don't know. In his journal, Magnus said something about the Northside Star?"

At this, Johnny smiled wide, though his breathing was growing even more labored. "That sly son of a bitch..." His head fell limp against the fridge; he wasn't trying to hold it up anymore. "Check the attic," he croaked. He took a final breath, and then his chest went still, a peaceful smile stretched across his gore-covered face.

Chyann stared hard at his dead body, hot tears welling in her eyes. *At least he's with his family now*, she thought.

CHAPTER ELEVEN

WELLINGTON THEATER WAS A monster of a building, stretching and twisting as if it were alive. It loomed over Chyann, Ryan, and Willy even when they were still hundreds of feet away.

The moon glowed bright, peeking out from the clouds above and illuminating the site ahead. Construction vehicles and other equipment had been parked all around–most notably a wrecking ball suspended by a crane. The wrecking ball was next to a fence, which Chyann and the boys had already begun to climb. It had been shut and locked, blocking access to the lot.

As Chyann dropped down to the other side, she caught sight of more work vehicles and some tractors.

There was even a truck with a concrete mixer on the back parked nearby.

Honestly, Wellington had never had much of a parking lot. It had had what was left of a sidewalk wrapping around the building, but the actual grounds had been made up mostly of dirt. Not now, though. Wooden beams lined the ground of what Chyann assumed would be a proper parking lot in the future.

"This place is huge," Willy said. "How the hell are we gonna find our way around in there?"

"We'll figure it out," Ryan replied. "Let's hurry and save Bobby before Woody finds that heart."

About a minute of running got them across the lot. Soon they reached the double doors at the front entrance, finding the stone stairs there in pieces. Chyann guessed years of no maintenance had rendered them as broken as the rest of the building. Ryan took the lead, pushing on the doors. They *creaked* open, and the trio stepped inside.

Dust fell from the ceiling of the theater's main hall, drifting through the stuffy air like snow. Chyann glanced around, searching for any sign of Bobby and Woody, and incomprehensible voices sounded from somewhere deep within the building.

"What's that?" Ryan whispered.

"Sounds like… talking," Willy whispered back.

As they listened further, one of the voices screeched, "*No!*" Chyann recognized the cry immediately. She didn't have a shred of doubt regarding who it belonged to: Bobby Fleck. She turned toward

Ryan and Willy, and the expressions on their faces showed they had come to the same realization.

"It came from back there," Ryan said, pointing to the end of the main hall. The trio hurried past broken furniture, discarded trash, and a fallen chandelier.

They reached the dark hallway and began tiptoeing down the stairs, the voices growing louder. As they approached a now-uncovered doorway on the right, its door broken and lying on the floor ahead, Chyann noticed a small hole in the wall. *The boys must have missed that*, she thought.

Chyann tapped Ryan and Willy on the shoulders and motioned to the hole. Then, very carefully, she peeked into it.

In the next room, Bobby was searching through debris along the floor. Tears ran down his cheeks as he moved old boards and other bits of rubble aside.

"Hurry up," Woody demanded from somewhere nearby. "We've got a lot of ground to cover." The dummy giggled before continuing. "Well, *you* do."

Chyann tilted her head to the right, and Woody came into view. The wall behind Woody had been smashed in, revealing another section of the theater. And, more importantly, another gateway into the room Woody and Bobby were standing in. *Maybe we can go around and catch Woody from behind.* The dummy stood close to Bobby, a blood-stained butcher knife in hand. Because of how small he was, it almost looked as if he were clutching a sword.

That must be the knife he used on Johnny, Chyann thought, her gut clenching. She stepped away from the peephole, swallowing back the sour vomit threatening to spew from her lips.

As Chyann collected herself, Willy leaned on the wall and pressed an eye against the hole to see inside. As he did so, an impossibly loud groan sounded all around them. Before anyone could react, the wall was moving.

Willy fell alongside the wall as it tipped inward and crashed to the floor, and the deafening sounds of brick and plaster collapsing echoed across the building.

Chyann's heart nearly stopped. *Dammit! Now Woody knows someone's here!* She peered through a cloud of dust, spotted two glowing purple orbs, and froze. Woody was glaring at them through the mess. His gaze fell on Willy, who was sprawled out over the wreckage. Willy offered a guilty smile–the same look he gave teachers when caught red-handed in the midst of a practical joke.

"Uhh… howdy?" Willy said.

"*Howdy*," Woody snarled, and raised his knife. Willy jumped to his feet. All the while, Bobby seized a loose piece of wood.

The ten-year-old batted Woody across the head with his "weapon." Woody stumbled to the side. Bobby dropped the plank and sprinted for Chyann.

Just as Woody regained his balance and faced everyone, a groan echoed through the air. It came from the building, as if the fortification were alive and crying out in pain because of its freshly destroyed wall.

Cracks began to appear in the other walls around them. The beams above snapped under the pressure. "Everybody move!" Ryan screamed, but it was too late. The ceiling fell. Chyann watched as it crushed Woody, and then it trapped her in place.

Suddenly her vision was blocked by dust and debris. And after that, darkness.

Chyann opened her eyes and looked around, her skull aching. Had something hit her on the head and knocked her unconscious? If that were the case, she hadn't been out for more than a minute or two, as multiple pieces of wreckage were still settling into their new positions on the ground. Her shoulder flared with familiar pain, a similar feeling erupting in her left leg.

There was a cough from somewhere nearby, but Chyann couldn't see anyone else.

"Guys?" Ryan called, his voice anxious.

"I'm here," Willy responded.

Chyann tried to reply next, but the only thing that came out was a hoarse croak. All the dust in the air must have affected her voice.

Ryan chuckled. "Way to bring the house down, Will."

"You know me," Willy said. "Sometimes I party too hard."

"Chy? Bobby?" Ryan continued, and Chyann sat up to examine her leg. She tried to speak again, but her voice was still too soft.

"You okay, kid?" Willy asked.

A few weak coughs. "I think so," Bobby answered.

Chyann tried to say something once more, finally finding her words. "I'm over here."

"Over where?" Ryan asked. "I don't see you."

She opened her mouth to talk but started hacking up what tasted like dirt. All the while, she realized several wooden beams had landed on her left leg. She pushed a few of them off. However, when she tried to move the limb, severe pain rivaling that of her stab wound shot through it. "I... I don't think I'm with you guys," she said with a groan.

"Wait," Willy started, "you mean... Are you a ghost?"

"What? No!" Chyann exclaimed. "I mean I'm on the other side."

"So, you *are* a ghost?"

"Will, shut up," Ryan chimed in. "She means on the other side of the cave-in."

"Ohh."

Soon Chyann heard wood and brick being tossed about, the debris before her shifting.

"We'll have you outta there any minute," Ryan said.

"No, stop!" she shouted. "If this place is really falling apart, moving stuff could trigger another hunk of the floor to fall in."

"Well, what else are we supposed to do?" Ryan replied. "Find a way around?"

"Find a way up," she told him. "I think I can make it back to the main hall from here. Just find some stairs, and we'll meet on one of the higher floors."

Ryan paused for a moment before replying. "Are you sure you're gonna be okay flying solo for a minute?"

"Honestly, no." Another wave of agony surged through her leg. "But I don't have much of a choice."

"Right. See you soon?"

"Sooner." Silence followed Chyann's answer, but she was pretty sure she heard them walk away. She was alone now, her leg still trapped under more debris. Thankfully, she could probably move all the rubble on her own.

After shoving a cinder block and some broken wood away, she found the culprit behind her pain. A large wooden shard had impaled the side of her leg, right below her knee. Moving the limb inward made it surge with new hurt. As she tried to shift around, she felt the muscles tighten around the foreign object, the sensation giving her a peculiar sense of terror. It was the kind of fear you experience when something new and strange has happened, and all you can think is, *I don't like that.*

This was going to be difficult, but if she wanted to get out of here and meet up with her friends, she was going to have to fix herself up. And that meant she needed to remove the shard.

Chyann touched the wood as gently as possible, but still her leg flooded with a pain even greater than that of her shoulder wound. Static trailed up from her toes, toward her left thigh. *Come on*, she thought. *Like a bandaid...*

An idea struck her, a shaky breath escaping her lips. Ryan owed her a shopping trip when this was over.

She removed her jacket and set it aside, then pulled off her white T-shirt. It wasn't too filthy, aside from some dust that had made it past her jacket and onto the collar. She twisted the shirt, put it in her mouth, and bit down. *Now for the hard part.*

She grabbed the shard. Throbbing pain beat through her leg in rhythm with her heart, speeding up as she tightened her grip on the wood. She pulled on it, gently, but she could feel it refusing to move. Boy, she could feel it. Despite the cloth in her mouth, her cries echoed across the room. She worried they might even be loud enough to further disrupt the building, causing more of it to collapse.

Hardening her resolve, she pulled at the shard once more. She tugged on it again and again, and the more she did so, the more potent her agony became. She jerked on it a final time, putting all her strength into it, ignoring the hurt that followed. Screaming, she wiggled the wood free from her leg. Blood spurted from the fresh wound, and she chucked the shard into the darkness.

Her whole body was shaking now, her senses engulfed by the extraordinary pain pulsing through her limb. It felt as if her blood were on fire.

The hardest part is over, she thought, spitting out the shirt. She untwisted the fabric, tore it into two pieces, and wrapped one of them around her thigh above the injury. Then she tied the second around the wound itself. It didn't help the pain, but she needed to stop the bleeding. She snatched her jacket, threw it on, and zipped it all the way up to cover herself, before attempting to stand.

At first she couldn't keep her balance, but once she could, she made sure to stand on her good leg. All the while, she allowed the bad limb to hover slightly above the floor. Putting any weight on it sent shock waves through her. Consequently, she had to hop/limp rather than actually walk. She put her hand against the wall to keep her balance, but she was careful not to press too hard on it. At this point, it seemed a gust of wind could knock over this death trap of a building.

With her free hand, she reached into her pocket, pulled out her cell phone, and switched on the flashlight to illuminate her path. Moving from one place to the next was happening slower than she would have liked, but she couldn't go any faster.

Finally, she made it to the main hall. She'd almost fallen twice on the way up, but thankfully she'd managed to catch herself both times.

She hobbled toward the stairwell that led to the higher floors. Once she arrived at the bottom, she spotted a metal rail bolted into the wall. Maybe it could help her travel more quickly up the stairs?

She grasped the railing as firmly as she could. The cool metal against her hot, sweaty palm was a welcome sensation. She began hopping up the stairs, and soon she arrived at the top. *That was faster than expected*, she thought. *Not that I'm complaining.*

She couldn't go any higher, as the next stairwell had caved-in beforehand and the debris blocked her way up. Her only option was to head down the long hallway on this level so she could get to the stairwell on the other side.

Tags and messages were spray-painted everywhere. The velvet decor was torn apart, the shredded fabric dangling loosely from the walls and ceiling. Portraits coated with ages of dust–ones that had surely once hung proudly on the walls–were scattered about the floor.

Chyann limped down the hall, her flashlight cutting through the dust-filled air. She glanced at many of the portraits she passed, and although they were covered with grime, she could still make out some of their key details. One featured a pair of twin sisters. Another displayed a round-faced man and his dalmation.

She couldn't really see a lot of the other portraits, but when she made it to the end of the hall, she had no problem seeing the ones there. Many of them had Woody and a younger Johnny Jamison pictured.

The sight of those two faces gave Chyann a pit in her stomach. She decided to keep her head down until she was out of the hall, but something caught her attention just before she made it to the next stairwell.

All over one of Johnny and Woody's portraits, a message was spray-painted in white: *The show must go on.* Chyann stopped for a second to look at it, then exited the hallway and started her trek up the next set of stairs.

She wasn't quite as lucky with this staircase as she had been with the last, as this one's railing was almost completely disconnected from the wall. Even the slightest bit of pressure sent it bobbing up and down. To balance herself on her way to the top, she had to place her hand against the wall instead. The stairs creaked as she climbed, and she was afraid she might fall through the floor. *Nothing about this place is safe. No wonder it's getting knocked down.*

She reached the top of the stairs and found herself in another hallway. This one was more condensed and was lined with rooms. Some of the rooms' doors had been knocked to the floor, while others were barely hanging on to their hinges. There was more graffiti in here, too. *Lies* was written on the wall to her right, the "i" missing because it had been sprayed onto a door that was now on the ground. *They knew* surrounded another old portrait, one of a man Chyann didn't recognize. *They saw* was painted in orange over said portrait, a stark contrast to the rest of the words, which were all in white.

She turned her light to examine the other side of the hall, where she met another chilling message: *They saw everything.* The words were painted over and over on the wall and had been shaped into a giant eye. Compared to the other graffiti, the eye was colossal, and at its very center was another sentence, this one in bright-red paint: *Beware those who watch from the shadows.*

Chyann shivered, limping past the graffiti, and finally arrived at a door that hadn't fallen off its hinges.

The metal plate on it read *Johnny L. Jamison*, and the white paint defacing the plate said *The man of the hour*. As she stepped toward the door, her heart beat so hard she thought it might explode.

With a dirty, sweat-covered hand, she reached out and pushed the door in. Apparently it hadn't been as secure as she'd initially thought–only the bottom hinges were still connected to the wall, and it dragged along the floor. Despite this, it still opened wide enough for her to walk through without much hassle.

The room on the other side looked a lot like the hallway behind her–coated with dust, broken and knocked-over furniture. *The show must go on* had been painted on the far-right wall. Opposite to the eerie message was a portrait of Johnny and Woody, except Woody's face had been carved away.

What really caught her attention, however, was the fireplace. It was large enough to walk into, and it wasn't until she hobbled closer that she realized a safe door was located inside of it. *What the hell?* she thought. *Is that for storing important goods, or does it lead to some kind of secret room? Also, how hasn't it fallen through the floor by now? This place is practically made of paper-mache.*

She shined her light at the safe door and saw the dial was gone. Orange dust filled the space where it should have been, and when Chyann pulled the door open with a loud *creak*, she saw that the inside was completely rusted through. *That's weird... right? Do things rust from the inside out like that?* She peered down at the ground and saw a square shape in the rust—one roughly the size of Woody's trunk. Now things were starting to make sense. This must be the secret room where Johnny had trapped Woody all those years ago.

Chyann turned around to leave, but another streak of white caught her eye. There was more paint on the inside of the door, but it wasn't like the rest of the graffiti. It hadn't been spray-painted on; it appeared to have been brushed on. That wasn't what made her blood run cold, though.

On the inside of the safe door, someone had painted a large triangle with an eye in the center. The eye was slightly larger than the triangle, its ends sticking out on the sides. Chyann raised a hand, gently running her fingers across the triangle. *I've seen this before...* She recalled the night she'd fallen off her bike on her way home from babysitting Bobby. She had seen this exact symbol on an old building. But what was it doing here? It had to have been painted on before the door had been sealed. She stumbled back, her stomach twisting and turning, though she wasn't sure whether her nausea had come from the thousand-year-old dust floating through the air or her own racing thoughts. She leaned against the stone of the fireplace, trying to catch her breath.

"Quite a sight, huh?" a familiar voice said.

She gasped in reply, feeling as though the air in her lungs had been sucked out, and looked up to see Woody's short silhouette standing in the room's main doorway.

The dummy held up his kitchen knife. He motioned around the room with the blade. "I always liked performing more than I initially thought I would. People practically worshiped me, and all I had to do was sit on some poor sap's lap and tell jokes." He took a few steps toward her. "Speaking of jokes, here's one for the pretty girl in the front row." He lowered his weapon, his irises glowing a fierce violet. Chyann chanced a glance around the room, spotted the massive portrait against the wall next to her.

"What do you have in common with Johnny Boy's kids?" Woody growled, edging closer to her. "Nothing at all... *yet.*" He raised the blade. She seized the edges of the portrait and shoved it on top of him. He toppled to the floor beneath the sudden weight, and she started limping away as fast as she could.

Her foot caught on the side of the frame. She stuck out her bad leg to catch herself, but pain jolted through it. She fell to the floor.

A noise like fabric tearing sounded from behind her. She glanced over her shoulder, saw Woody cutting through the back of the canvas. He pushed his head through with an angry yell.

Chyann struggled, trying to scramble to her feet. She reached out for something to help pull herself up, and her fingers tightened around a piece of the wall. She wasn't sure what it was exactly. Too difficult to see in the chaos. Whatever it was–a piece of the wall's framing, maybe–it held strong. Strong enough for her to pull herself into a standing position.

She looked back, readjusting her phone so she

could see more clearly. Woody had yet to free himself of the portrait, and he hacked wildly at it with the blade. Despite the agony in her leg, Chyann started to limp-run out of the room. Her new wound flared with every step she took, but the farther she went, the easier running became. Was adrenaline taking over?

A sharp *snap* sounded from behind her as she hurtled into the hallway. "Get back here!" Woody screamed. Then she heard footsteps drumming against the floor, getting closer and closer... *I'm never going to outrun him like this!* she thought. *I'm too slow!*

The flashlight on her phone illuminated another open door up ahead, revealing a stairwell going upward. She lunged into the doorway and slammed the door shut behind her before Woody could follow. *Thank God this one isn't broken*, she thought, pressing herself against it to keep it shut. However, she needed to find something else to block it so she could get away.

She scanned the immediate area, finding a wooden chair strung with dusty cobwebs to the left. *Perfect.*

Something slammed into the door behind her. She screamed, her heart pounding. "Knock, knock," Woody said from the other side. The knob turned, the door sliding open and closed. If Chyann hadn't been pressing it shut, she was sure it would have swung open completely. Woody paused his assault on the door momentarily, and she reached for the chair with one hand. *This is it.*

Something sharp sank into the back of her arm, the one still pressed against the door. She cried out, hot pain searing through the limb, and looked back. Woody had pierced through the door with the knife. He'd stabbed her in the process.

"You're supposed to say 'who's there'!" he yelled. He yanked the blade back and resumed banging against the door. Ignoring her new pain as best she could, Chyann chanced reaching for the chair again. Her fingers brushed the top of it, and she pulled it toward herself and shoved it underneath the doorknob. Thankfully, the effort was enough to keep the door blocked for now, although Woody was still trying to get through.

Chyann hurried up the stairwell. *I have to try and get a head start, at least,* she thought. After all, as Woody slammed himself against the door a few more times, the chair's legs began to splinter.

She hobbled up as fast as she could. When she reached the top, she didn't hesitate to start up the next flight. Below, Woody broke open the door with a loud *crack*. He chuckled sadistically, the sound of his shoes hitting the stairs echoing behind her.

Panic gripped Chyann's senses. Woody was close, and there wasn't anything left between them to give her the upper hand.

She reached the top of the second flight of stairs and stumbled through the open doorway leading to the twelfth floor. It was lined with rooms and defaced with spray paint, just as the floors below were. But that couldn't be right, could it? Wasn't the top floor supposed to be an attic?

Woody cackled from somewhere behind her. "You can't run, you can't hide. What's a girl to do?"

She hurdled farther down the hall, glancing over her shoulder to see that Woody had made it to the top of the stairs. Despite his short stature and the wonky way his boneless legs carried him, he was quite fast. In no time at all he'd begun to gain ground on her. *If I can't escape him*, she thought, *I'm going to have to fight him.*

She looked ahead, scanning her surroundings as she ran. Broken-off pieces of the walls. Old picture frames. Fallen doors. Nothing that would serve as a reliable weapon–not as far as she could tell. She couldn't do much fighting with a bum leg, either.

Just as Chyann began to lose hope, her phone's flashlight illuminated what she needed. *Attic Access* was plated above a doorway to her left. Like most of the building's rooms, the actual door was disconnected from the frame. She could see the stairwell on the other side, which appeared to be as tight as the doorway itself. She hurried in and maneuvered herself upward.

The stairwell was so narrow she could touch the walls on either side if she wanted, and the flights were only five or six stairs high before changing direction and leading into new ones. Thanks to the somewhat stable railing, she also managed to swing herself up the steps quickly.

Up and up she climbed. After the sixth or seventh set, she began to wonder if she was heading for the attic or the top of the world.

Several more minutes ticked by before she reached the attic. There was another doorway, but unlike the one below, this one was still intact. She pushed against it, but it refused to open, and when she looked down she realized why. There was a rusty padlock above the knob, keeping the room sealed shut.

The padlock had obvious signs of abuse; it was clear people had tried to break it, as there were many scratches on the steel. No one had been successful, though, because Chyann still couldn't get in. She tugged on the padlock with her free hand, but it held firm regardless of age and damage. There wasn't anything else inside the stairwell, either, so she didn't have something to strike the obstacle with.

Regardless, she needed in there. And to do that, she had to bite the bullet. A swift kick would hopefully snap it open.

After a quick deliberation, she decided she had to kick the lock using her bad leg. It would be much harder to get a well-aimed hit if she balanced on it instead. This was the only way.

She stood on her good leg, getting her balance in order. And, after taking a deep breath, she delivered the strongest kick she could muster to the side of the padlock.

The pain that followed was the worst she'd experienced yet; it felt as though her leg were pinned between two building-sized hammers. It maddened her, sent her reeling. She screamed, but the sound was only white noise to her own ears.

Some time passed. She wasn't sure how long exactly. Eventually, the pain subsided enough for her to compose herself. She looked up at the door to see the padlock was broken. The top half still hung from the door, but the bottom half had fallen to the floor.

She slowed her breathing and listened closely, trying to discover whether Woody was close. She couldn't hear anything to suggest he was around, though. However, since she'd screamed, he'd probably find her soon.

Chyann struggled to her feet and limped to the door. She pulled away what remained of the lock and tossed it aside, then pushed herself against the door and stumbled into the attic.

CHAPTER TWELVE

T HE AIR IN THE attic smelled different than the rest of the theater. It was heavier, mustier. Chyann guessed it had something to do with the fact that nobody had been up here recently.

Furniture covered with dirty sheets had been scattered everywhere. In fact, the way it had all been placed reminded her of a maze. She hurried down the paths constructed between shelves and chairs.

Somewhere in the attic was a clue that would lead Chyann to Woody's heart. That had to be the case–that was what Johnny had told her. But where was she supposed to start? *There's a thousand different places it could be*, she thought. *The attic makes up a whole floor of the building.*

Another clue–the one Ryan and Willy had mentioned earlier–came back to her. The North Star. *Is the heart on the north side of the attic?*

She lowered her phone and opened a compass app on it. North was to her right. She turned that way and noticed the window overhead. It was circular and had a cross framing, the moon shining in from outside.

It was through this window that Chyann saw the star. The North Star in the sky above.

She limped over to the window and began her search, soon discovering a small, rust-covered box sitting atop one of the window's support beams. It was out of reach, but that was nothing a chair couldn't fix.

She dragged the nearest chair closer. Bum leg and all, she climbed on top of it, then reached up to grab the box. With trembling fingers she seized it and pulled it down to examine. It seemed quite old–she guessed it had been well-worn even before it had been left in an attic for almost thirty years. There was a tiny latch on the front of it, affixed with a miniature padlock.

Chyann lowered herself into a seated position. She dusted off the box's remaining cobwebs before bashing it against the chair's armrest. The little padlock broke instantly, and she pried the box open to inspect what was inside.

The heart was bigger than she'd expected–a mass of dried flesh stained black, with white veins riddled across the surface. She illuminated the object with her cell phone, exhaling an exhausted breath of relief. *This has to be it*, she thought. *I found the heart!*

Her excitement was short-lived, however. The heart began to expand and contract, beating slowly despite not being connected to anything. Chyann gasped, ready to set the box down, when something blunt and hard struck her in the side of the head. She lost grip of the box and tumbled off the chair.

Her cheek hit the floor, then the rest of her did, too. Her vision blurred, her ears ringing. Bright light stung her eyes. It was only when her vision finally cleared that she saw it was because of her phone's flashlight. She tried to lift herself up off the filthy floor, but something pressed against her head, pinning her down. Woody's sinister laugh filled the room. "Way to go, kiddo," he said. "You won the scavenger hunt! Thanks for bein' such a good sport."

Something pounded against the floor.

Thud. Thud. Thud.

The heart must have fallen out of the box when she'd dropped it. It pulsated only a few feet away from her. Behind it, a mirror rested against some boxes. Through the glass's grime, Chyann saw her reflection. Woody had a foot pressed against her skull and the knife in hand. The blade gleamed as he rose it high above his head. "Here's yer prize, kid!"

As Chyann watched Woody bring the weapon down in the mirror, a figure leapt into view behind the dummy, and a shovel swung out from the darkness. The metal spade connected with Woody's head. It batted him away like a baseball, sending him flying into a pile of boxes off to the side. They crashed to the floor all around him.

"How's that for a knock on wood?" Willy said as he lowered the shovel. Ryan and Bobby appeared behind him, and Ryan hurried over to Chyann. He helped her up, and she wrapped him into a tight hug, relief enveloping her senses.

"Am I glad to see you guys!" she exclaimed.

"Likewise," Ryan replied. "Now let's get the hell outta here." He grabbed her phone and Woody's still-beating heart, then helped her over to Willy and Bobby. Together, the four of them hurried through the winding maze of furniture until they reached another entrance to the attic; Chyann knew this one was different from the one she'd used because it wasn't nearly as cramped, a burnt-out *Exit* sign bolted to the ceiling above it.

They sped through the doorway down into a rickety old stairwell. *This must be how Ryan, Willy, and Bobby got up here*, Chyann thought. Willy rested the shovel over his shoulder and led them down. "We gotta take these kinda slow," he said. "They don't feel very–" Before he could finish, the step he was standing on broke, and he fell with it. He caught himself on the railing and managed to pull himself back up to safety, but the rest of the stairs rumbled loudly before crumbling and collapsing just as the first one had. Soon they were a pile of lumber two floors below. "So, uh, yeah," Willy continued, his voice shaking, although Chyann could tell he was trying to play it cool. "That's what I was afraid of."

"Now what?" Ryan asked.

"I got up here through a tighter staircase on the eastern side of the attic," Chyann said. "We can go back and use that. They're much sturdier than these were, anyway."

A loud *creeeaaak* sounded from all around. Chyann looked up to see a support beam snapping in half. Bits of the ceiling began to shower down on their heads, and everyone darted backward. A massive strip of wood plunged from the roof and rammed into the space in front of them, the cloudy night sky now on full display above them. "We gotta hurry!" Ryan shouted. "Before the whole place comes down on top of us!"

They dashed for the other entrance, but dust swirled around them like a sandstorm, blinding them. Suddenly a pair of glowing purple eyes sliced through the muck, and then the rest of Woody came into view. He still had the knife, and a deep crack traveled up the right side of his face like a lightning bolt. "A shovel, really?" he said, chuckling, and Chyann watched in horror as the fracture on his face began sealing itself shut. Before she knew it, it was completely gone. Woody raised the blade and started toward them. "You guys *crack me up*."

Ryan yanked Chyann and Bobby backward and shielded everyone with his arms. As Woody stepped closer to them, they backed away. Chyann caught sight of the piece of the ceiling that had fallen in; it had formed a kind of makeshift ramp that led out to the roof.

"The roof," she said, and Ryan turned sharply toward her. She jerked her head at the piece of lumber leading outside. "If we can't go down," she continued, "then we go up." Nobody argued with her. Willy stepped in front of everyone, using the shovel to guard them as they swung around and scrambled up the planking.

Ryan helped Chyann up, Bobby behind them. When she was almost outside, cold wind blasted her in the face, crept through the crevices of her jacket and chilled the bare skin beneath. The wind was fierce, and it threatened to grow worse. As they stepped onto the roof, a gust nearly knocked them over.

They reclaimed their balance, and Chyann glanced over her shoulder, looking out at the glimmering lights of Twilight Peak. She couldn't see directly over the edge of the theater from where she stood now, but she could see enough to know that if she fell, it was a long way to the ground.

Willy hurried up the "ramp" next. Ryan helped him out, then began ushering everyone away from the newly formed hole. "Let's hope the roof isn't as fragile as the rest of the building," he said.

"It's lasted this long," Willy responded hopefully. Together, the four of them watched the cavity they'd used to get up here.

Just as Chyann knew he would, Woody climbed into view. "It won't last for much longer, though," he chirped. "The same could be said for all of you." He raised his knife and stomped forward. Willy stepped back, swinging the shovel at the doll. Woody ducked beneath the attack. Willy stumbled to the side. Woody slammed his head into Willy's shin with a hollow *clunk*.

Willy dropped to a knee. Woody slashed the blade at him. He lost grip of the shovel, reeling back, blood squirting from a cut on his arm. Ryan released his hold on Chyann and rushed toward the fight.

Woody snatched up the shovel with his free hand. He swung it at Ryan, and it connected with the boy's skull. Ryan crumpled into a heap, the heart rolling out of his pocket.

"And here I was worried that Magnus's grandson was gonna be an issue," Woody said. He spotted the heart, wiggled his eyebrows at Chyann, and tossed the shovel off the side of the roof. It clanged against something far below.

Chyann bolted toward the black, fleshy organ, but her bad leg gave out, and she fell face-first into the tin and clay tiles of the old roof. Bobby rushed to her side and grabbed her arm, holding her tight.

Woody scooped up his heart and inspected it. "Yes... *yes!*" His amethyst irises glowed brighter as the organ began beating rapidly. Sparking energy surged from it, through Woody, electricity arcing across his limbs.

Woody dropped the knife. His eyebrows lowered over the tops of his eyes, and he glared at Chyann. "It's time for the main event!"

Willy leapt to his feet. He rushed toward Woody, ready to meet the dummy head-on. Woody raised his arms in a showman's stance. "For my first trick, I'll require an assistant." He jerked an arm at Willy. "You there, sir!" Green electricity fired from his palm.

The current struck Willy in the center of his chest, sending a visible shock wave of light across his body. The force knocked him off his feet, throwing him backward as though he'd been fired from a cannon. He slammed into the roof. The rotting shingles around him crumbled apart, and he fell into the darkness below.

Chyann's chest tightened. She gasped, trying to catch her breath, but no air came. *Is Willy… No, he can't! He's…* "Willy!" she managed to scream, her voice hoarse.

Ryan was back on his feet in a flash. He charged toward Woody. "Don't make me laugh," Woody said. He threw a hand up and fired a stream of energy at Ryan. The electricity hit Ryan, but it also formed what seemed to be some sort of hold on Ryan's body.

Ryan cried out in pain as Woody lifted him into the air using the magic, and Chyann's blood went frigid as ice. Ryan and Willy were her best friends in the whole world. Not only that, but sometimes it felt as if they *made up* her whole world. And they were in more trouble than ever before. If something happened to them…

The thought made her shake, made her head spin. She felt as though she were stuck in the middle of an earthquake and a tornado simultaneously. Ryan and Willy were going to be killed right before her eyes, and she was doing nothing.

Ryan yelled again, snapping Chyann from her trance, and she looked up at him. Cuts began to appear on his cheeks and neck. "Tell Magpie that ol' Woody said *howdy*," Woody hissed. Ryan screamed a third time, somehow even louder now.

Ryan's shrieks and Woody's words were enough to get Chyann up. The pain in her leg throbbed with every movement, but she fought against it and rushed forward.

She seized Woody by the scruff of his neck and lifted him off the ground. With her other hand she grabbed the heart. She tried to pull it away from Woody, but he held firm. "Hey, hands off the merchandise!" he said, thrashing against her. His beam of electricity dissipated, and Ryan fell down onto the roof.

Chyann tried yanking the organ away a second time, but Woody kept a strong grip on it. "Let go!" he screeched.

"No," Chyann stated through gritted teeth. "I'm done being afraid of you."

Woody laughed long and loud. It was an obnoxious sound, and it made Chyann even angrier than before. "You don't need to worry about *fearing* me," he replied. The heart glowed bright in their shared grasp, and a stinging sensation traveled up her arm. She dropped Woody and stumbled back, agony flaring in her leg. She tripped over the pain and landed hard on her bottom.

Woody climbed to his feet. "You're all gonna be dead long before you need to be." He turned toward

Bobby and took a few steps forward, raising a hand. The ten-year-old was involuntarily thrown into the air and flown to Woody's side. Chyann reached for the boy, but he was far out of reach. "Except for you, of course," Woody said to Bobby. "I've got big plans for you. You're gonna be my new start."

There was a childlike glee in Woody's voice that made Chyann's skin crawl. "What?" she asked.

Woody flicked his eyes to the side to look at her without moving his head. "If you think my magic tricks are good now…" He paused, turned to face her. Leaned closer as Bobby writhed in the air. "Just wait until you see me in a body that isn't made of wood."

Despite everything she'd seen and learned today, Woody's words still shocked Chyann. She froze in place, all other thoughts derailing as one took over her mind. *He's gonna transfer his consciousness into Bobby's body.*

Woody's gaze remained fixed on her. He stepped toward her, only a few feet away now. "That just leaves me with you, girly. What to do, what to do…" He clicked his wooden teeth, his eyes going back and forth.

Chyann glanced over the edge of the building, desperate to find a way to stop Woody. She could make out tons of tractors and trucks below, but one vehicle in particular caught her eye. *The concrete truck*, she thought. *It's on?* The cylinder on the back of the vehicle was slowly rotating, and even from up here, Chyann could see the steady stream of fresh concrete it was pouring out into the readied pit. She squinted, saw the faint outline of a shovel beside the vehicle. *The shovel! It must have landed on something to start the mixer when Woody threw it off the roof,* she realized.

"Maybe I'll toss you off the side of the theater." Woody continued. "It'll be your big break. Only instead of in show business, it'll be on the *ground*."

Chyann had always thought it was silly how some people said light bulbs turning on represented new-found ideas. Now, though? She couldn't imagine a more perfect analogy as her mind lit up with what very well could be the only way to beat Woody at this point. *We don't destroy him. We* trap *him.*

She hissed out a long breath and glared daggers into Woody. "I like the way you think," she said, before wrapping her arms around him and rolling backward. Bobby fell from the air and crashed next to Ryan.

"Chy!" Ryan shouted desperately. There was nothing he could do, though. Before he had the chance to get to his feet, Chyann and Woody tumbled over the edge of the roof.

She relinquished her hold on the dummy so she could reach out and grab something. With one hand she caught part of the theater's siding, her stomach lurching as she grasped it tight. Something seized her bad leg, and a noise like wood striking a hard surface sounded in the air.

"No!" Woody screeched. "You stupid little brat!"

She looked down to see Woody's heart falling thirty feet below, the lavender glow emanating from it fading as it plummeted down. Soon its light disappeared completely.

"You're gonna pay for this ridiculous stunt," Woody yelled. He began climbing up her leg as if it were a rope in gym class. "Don't you get it yet? I'm invincible! You can't get rid of me." He slammed a palm onto her leg wound and squeezed. A scream erupted from her lips as fresh throbs and stings surged up and down the limb.

"Chy!" Ryann called from above. He was leaning over the edge, reaching for her. But he was just out of grasp.

More pain shot through her leg as Woody dug his fingers into the wrappings of her injury. She shrieked, trying to shake him loose.

Woody's hold on her slipped. He dropped down to her foot but clutched her ankle. For a moment, their eyes met. Then she kicked him in the face with her good foot. The force knocked one of his hands free of her ankle. He grunted angrily as she booted him again. "Well," he said, "ain't *this* a kick in the face?"

She delivered one last blow, and his head spun as he finally lost his grip on her. As he fell, he screamed.

It didn't take long for him to land in the pool of concrete next to the truck below. As he sank into the mixture, he looked up at her. But before he could hurl whatever cheesy line he had planned, the truck dumped more concrete on top of him, burying him entirely.

Chyann sighed in relief. There was no time to celebrate, though. The strain in her fingers clasping the building was becoming hard to ignore. She knew she couldn't hold on much longer.

"Chy, come on!" Ryan said. His extended hand was as close to her as he could manage without tumbling over the edge himself. She pressed her good leg against the building and caught a crevice in the wall with her shoe, planning to lift herself the tiniest bit using what leverage she could.

Mustering the last of her strength, Chyann leapt upward, snatching Ryan's hand. For a second it felt as if they were going to fall, but Ryan held fast and hauled her up to safety. "I gotcha," he assured her.

It took a lot of effort on Ryan's end, but soon Chyann was back on the roof. She threw her arms around his neck, enveloping him in a hug. "You good?" he asked into her shoulder.

She laughed into his before letting him go. "Ask me again tomorrow." They scooted away from the edge, and Bobby hurried over to Chyann to hug her as well. All the while, Ryan crawled over to the cavity in the roof Willy had fallen into.

"You did it, Chy," Bobby exclaimed as he embraced her.

"Yeah, I guess I did," she said.

Bobby let her go, his expression serious. "Now you're the hero."

At this, her heart warmed, and suddenly the chilly wind didn't feel so piercing on her skin anymore. She climbed to her feet and headed over to Ryan with Bobby in tow.

"Will, wake up!" Ryan shouted down into the hole. When Chyann got close enough to look inside, she saw Willy had landed in the attic. He was sprawled atop a heap of debris and sheet-covered furniture. His eyes were closed, his hands resting peacefully on his chest, his breathing slow and relaxed.

"Will," Chyann shouted.

Willy opened his eyes slightly. "What?" he asked irritably, as if she'd woken him from a great dream.

The corners of Chyann's mouth turned up in a big smile. She glanced at Ryan; he appeared to be just as relieved as she felt. "You okay?" Ryan asked Willy.

Willy flashed them the "okay" sign and offered a weak smile. "I'm over the freakin' moon."

EPILOGUE

CHYANN SAT BACK ON her bed, reading the last few pages of her mystery novel, the midday sun shining in through her bay windows. A few of them were open, allowing a gentle breeze into the room. She lifted a hand from the page to scratch the side of her head, careful not to ruin the bun she'd tied her hair up in earlier.

There was a twinge of pain in her leg, and she looked over at her still-healing shin. The wound was bound with fresh bandages–she'd rewrapped it eight times since Woody's defeat. She wore shorts and a tank top, an appropriate choice for such a warm day. She thought of cats sunbathing and realized she'd begun to understand why they found it so enjoyable.

She resumed reading after taking an extra pain med to dull her aches, then topped off the book's final page. The twist had blown her away, and the story itself had been rather enjoyable. One of the central themes was dealing with fear, and once the main character mastered this ability, he managed to solve the case.

Chyann huffed as she began to draw an alarming number of parallels between the story and her own recent experiences. Life was funny like that; it wasn't hard to see a bit of yourself in everything around you.

It had been roughly five days since she'd sent Woody into a well-paved grave, and hindsight brought some closure to a few of the insecurities she'd been facing these past few weeks. What did she even–

Her bedroom door swung open wildly. A dark shape leapt into her room at breakneck speed. It raised its arms and shouted, "Boo!"

She didn't scream. She hardly even moved. After a moment, she crossed her arms and turned to Willy, mustering the proudest smile she could manage. "That's the best you got?" she asked.

Willy lowered his arms. "Awe, c'mon Chy. There's no way you knew I was comin.'"

"I did, actually," she countered. "I saw you walking up to the house a minute ago." She leaned to her left, picked up her laptop, and flipped the device open to show Willy a set of security-camera feeds revealing footage of the front door and several other angles of her house from outside.

Willy nodded and shrugged. "See, now that I know those are there, I'm gonna have to try harder next time."

Chyann rolled her eyes and set her laptop aside. "Yeah, okay Will."

The boy ran a hand through his mohawk and took a seat on the bed next to her legs. "What did the doc say?"

"Well, Ed finally woke up. Might still have some muscle pains, but he could be home as early as next week."

Willy smiled, nodding at her leg. "I meant about you."

"Oh…" Her cheeks grew warm, but she wasn't sure whether it was from the heat coming in through her windows or if she was blushing. "I'm fine. I just can't walk much." She gestured toward the crutches set against her bedside table. "Not unassisted, anyway."

Willy hopped to his feet. "Right. Well, get comfy." He strolled over to her bedroom door. "I'll be back in twenty with Ryan and Sadie, burgers from Larry's, and a stack of movies."

Chyann grinned, mulling over the idea. She had just finished her book, and she hadn't eaten anything yet today. Friends, food, and fun sounded like heaven on earth. "That sounds like a great idea," she said.

"Well, duh. Of course it does." Willy hung on the door. "It was *my* idea." She chuckled, and Willy pointed at her, offering her his signature mischievous smirk. "Don't go anywhere while I'm gone, Limpy."

Chyann snatched a pillow from her bed and chucked it at Willy. He ducked around the corner and started down the stairs. "Where am I gonna go?" she shouted at him, laughing. His only reply was the front door opening and closing downstairs, so she settled back against her pillows and stared out her windows at the bright, beautiful day outside.

RYAN FLIPPED THE light switch on and proceeded down the stairs leading to his basement, holding a small, rust-covered box under an arm as he descended. Mist curled and shimmered over the left side of his face, forming half of Boss's face.

When he reached the bottom of the steps, Ryan could see that dust coated everything in the basement, but it was still leagues cleaner than Wellington Theater. *I need to tidy things up down here*, he thought. *One of these days.*

"Chyann certainly rose to the challenge back on the roof of the theater," Boss mentioned. "I've noticed she's adept at hand-to-hand combat for her age."

"Yeah," Ryan replied. "Ever since her sister vanished, her mom enrolled her in all kinds of stuff to keep her safe. Track, self-defense, the works. You name it, Chy's done it."

"She would have fit in well back in my village." Sadness laced Boss's words.

Ryan's shoulders slumped. "I'm sorry."

Boss didn't respond, and Ryan continued past

the basement's run-down kitchen and headed toward Grandpa Magnus's old bedroom, a familiar ache pulling at his heart. It hurt to be in there, but it would only be for a few minutes at most. After that, he'd be at Chy's for the rest of the day.

When he reached the door, he pushed it open and turned on the light, then strode over to the closet and pulled out Grandpa's old trunk. "You were right before, you know," he said to Boss, unlocking the trunk and popping the lid open. "Chyann didn't wanna be left behind."

Boss only nodded, and Ryan peered down at the trunk's contents–the knife, the journal, and an assortment of monster-hunting gear. He took the rust-covered box out from under his arm and opened it next. Woody's black heart lay lifeless inside.

"It's crazy," he continued, "that something as dangerous as Woody was hiding right under our noses for so long. And we had no idea..."

Boss finally spoke. "It is rather concerning."

"I wonder what other secrets are buried in this town." Ryan closed the box that contained Woody's heart and dropped it into Grandpa's chest.

A CHARRED-BLACK mess landed on the desk in front of Legacy. He couldn't discern exactly what he was staring at, so he tilted his head up at Heritage, who had entered his office with the object. "What is this?"

"That," Heritage said, pointing at it, "is the remains of a teddy bear."

Legacy looked past Heritage to see Genesis, who stood at the doorway in silence. "A teddy bear?" Legacy repeated.

Heritage folded his arms behind his back. "Specifically, a teddy bear from the home that once housed Adella Williams."

Now *that* was an interesting detail. Could it mean... "Those children removed her from the building?" Legacy asked.

Heritage nodded. "There's no sign of her ghost anywhere. It appears she has finally moved on."

Legacy leaned back in his chair and cupped his chin with his palm. For many years he had been greatly confused as to why Adella had stuck around. They'd burnt her bones long ago–far from her grave, of course. They'd had to replace the remains with fakes after an incident with the nosy sheriff.

For one reason or another, the spirit of Adella had persisted, though. Sure, she could have been anchored to an item, but their many searches of the Williams property had never produced anything to support that theory. It impressed and worried Legacy all at the same time that the children had disposed of her. They'd accomplished what he hadn't been able to. How was he supposed to feel about that?

He disregarded the thought with a wave of his hand. A much more pressing matter required his attention. "And what of the situation at Wellington

Theater? Has the subject been located?" Heritage looked down as if in guilt.

Legacy's nostrils flared. He hated it when Heritage did that. It meant there was bad news, and it seemed all Heritage had done lately was bring him bad news.

"Unfortunately, sir, the subject has yet to be located," Heritage mumbled. He was young, new to the fold. Mistakes were inevitable for someone in his shoes. Legacy could only forgive so many mistakes, however. He pursed his lips and nodded in response.

"The subject," a new voice said, "is back at Wellington Theater." Legacy's attention shifted to Genesis. His voice was deep and rather raspy-sounding due to the respirator connected to the mask he wore.

Heritage turned back to Genesis. "And how would you know that?"

"Because," Genesis began, annoyance in his words, "I was doing your job while you were gone. I found the subject and tracked his movements."

"That's not fair! I was busy doing–"

Genesis cut him off. "The subject was buried in concrete beneath a new foundation at the site. He was dealt with by the very same children who helped Adella's spirit move on."

Now Genesis really had Legacy's attention. To hear that the children had defeated not one, but *two* supernatural threats? Clearly Magnus had had some sort of influence on them. It was amusing, really.

Legacy chuckled. "Even in death, the late and great Magnus Myers causes problems. Perhaps these children are more of a nuisance than I initially thought."

"What should we do?" Heritage inquired.

Legacy considered his options for a moment. The children were still his best lead to the source. They had all of Magnus's notes–the missing pieces to his puzzle. If they were as adventurous as they had begun to seem… "Continue watching them closely for me," Legacy ordered. "Report back on their actions, motives, friends. I want to know more about them."

Heritage bowed. "Of course, sir."

"Not you," Legacy snapped. Heritage looked up, his mouth agape. "Genesis will watch the children," Legacy said. "I want to know every little thing about them."

Genesis nodded and left the room without another word.

"Legacy, please," Heritage started. "I have been juggling many difficult tasks. There's only so much I can do."

"I'm well aware of that. Your job is arguably more important than watching the children, though." The confidence rushed back into Heritage's expression. "And you're correct," Legacy continued. "I have been assigning you much to do. Which is why you must now give your full attention to your current task. It is of the utmost importance."

Heritage nodded twice. Legacy leaned forward in his seat, making sure to keep his voice low as he uttered his next words. "I will not tolerate further failure. Our job is important, and if you cannot be trusted to uphold your promise to us, you will be removed."

Heritage hung his head. "Understood, sir." He exited the room.

Legacy was finally alone with his thoughts, and what thoughts they were. He thought of the children, of Adella Williams, and now of the recently freed sorcerer that lived within a ventriloquist dummy.

Not to mention there was that mysterious man who had murdered the cat-creature, and who had seemingly died in a building collapse. That man–he had *survived*. Survived, and then escaped the hospital holding him after assaulting a nurse there.

Oh, the conversations Legacy would have when his men finally found the strange survivor and sat him down in this very office.

Things had gotten very interesting, indeed.

TO BE CONTINUED
IN BOOK 4

MALEVOLENCE

WRITTEN BY
D.R. MILLS

WOODY THE DUMMY

*If you would like to follow D. R. Mills's journey or the **MONSTERS** series specifically, check out the author's official Twitter and Instagram accounts:*

- Instagram: @monsters_bookseries
- Twitter: @MonstersSeries
- Facebook: @Monsters/100067554032850
- TikTok: www.tiktok.com/@monstersseries

If you enjoyed the story, dont forget to leave a review on your preferred platform! Reviews help authors find more readers, and if you'd like D. R. Mills to be able to release books faster, reviews are the best way to support him.

ACKNOWLEDGMENTS

Well, well, well. If it isn't the end of another book. I sure hope this one didn't take as long to come out as the last one did. Either way, I hope it was worth the wait! This is one of my personal faves in the first season. So much development for Chyann, so many gruesome scenes across Twilight Peak, so many *cheesy* one-liners from Woody…

This one was longer than *The Girl Next Door*, and, as a result, it was a bit more work. But I think the final product came out awesome. I hope you enjoyed reading it as much as I loved writing it!

As usual, I couldn't have gotten this story into your hands without the help of some amazing people, and they deserve all the thanks in the world. (I guess a section at the end of the book will have to do for now.)

Ali! All you do for this series does not go unnoticed. You're basically a beta reader and editor all in one, and the love and effort you put into these books is rivaled only by my own. I will always be thankful for our friendship, and for the shine you put on each of these books before publication. *Especially that shine.* Lord knows they need it…

Emily! My beautiful wife! For always giving me ideas, and also space when I need it to finish these books. Thanks for letting me talk your ear off about whatever crazy ideas I have bouncing around in my head. It's definitely more fun than talking to myself.

Mom! You're *still* selling more copies of my own books than I am. That's just how it's working out for me, I guess. Thanks for the endless stream of support you've given me. If I make it big someday, I'll buy you a really nice chair as thanks. Okay, okay–maybe I'll get you more than *just* a really nice chair.

Crutches! I already dedicated this book to you. What more do you want? The foundation of the manuscript was built on some early feedback you gave me for the series. I hope it shows when you read the books.

Enchanted Ink! These formatters are phenomenal, and they knock it out of the park with every single book. Thanks for always being so patient with me and my many emails. I'll get the hang of this author thing someday. Probably.

The team at MiblArt! I need to thank these guys as well for being patient with me during our back-and-forths regarding book covers! I'm continuously happy with every piece I commission with the company, and I hope I can continue doing so.

And, of course, thank you to my *readers*. Whether you waited patiently for this book or happened to find a copy lying in an old box in the woods, I'm beyond grateful that you gave it a read. I hope you enjoyed it, and that you keep up with the series.

Speaking of the series, how long until the next book?

...Wait, that's your line. If all goes well, you should see some news regarding the next installment *very soon*. It definitely won't be another year. Publishing one book a year is dumb; in 2023 I'm shooting for three or four.

Hopefully I can follow-through with that goal so I don't look back on this note later and get angry with myself.

See you then.
–DRM

D. R. MILLS

is a young-adult horror author who is currently hard at work on his debut series, *MONSTERS*. He was born and raised in Wyoming, where he's still lurking around somewhere. When he isn't writing, he's playing video games a borderline unhealthy amount or spending time with his beautiful wife.

WWW.SEAOFINKPRESS.WORDPRESS.COM